THE CONSTANT COMPANION

MARION CHESNEY

THE CONSTANT
COMPANION

Thorndike Press • Chivers Press
Waterville, Maine USA   Bath, England

This Large Print edition is published by Thorndike Press, USA and by Chivers Press, England.

Published in 2001 in the U.S. by arrangement with Lowenstein Associates, Inc.

Published in 2001 in the U.K. by arrangement with the author.

U.S. Hardcover 0-7862-3634-5 (Romance Series Edition)
U.K. Hardcover 0-7540-4724-5 (Chivers Large Print)
U.K. Softcover 0-7540-4725-3 (Camden Large Print)

The text of this Large Print edition is unabridged.
Other aspects of the book may vary from the original edition.

Set in 16 pt. Plantin by PerfecType.

British Library Cataloguing in Publication Data available

Library of Congress Cataloging-in-Publication Data

Chesney, Marion.
   The constant companion / Marion Chesney.
      p. cm.
   ISBN 0-7862-3634-5 (lg. print : hc : alk. paper)
      1. Missing persons — Fiction. 2. Married women —
Fiction. 3. England — Fiction. 4. Large type books. I. Title.
PR6053.H4535 C66 2001
   823´.914—dc21   2001048034

For Sally and Michael Murphy
and their children, Conal and Gavin,
With Much Love

Chapter One

At ten o'clock in the morning, there is usually an uncanny quiet in the squares and streets of the West End of London. The workers have already gone to work, the jugglers, conjurers and raree men have not yet arrived, the servants are quietly engaged in their multitude of tasks and have no time to take the air, for some odd reason the tradesmen cease to cry their wares and fashionable London lies abed, sipping its morning chocolate, and lazily turns over the gilt-embossed invitation cards which have been presented with the breakfast tray.

One fine Wednesday morning in early spring was no exception to the rule. The sun shone from behind a high, thin layer of smoke, bathing the city in a warm golden glow. Not a breath of wind disturbed the calm, still order of the stately homes, ordered parks and squares where daffodils stood sentinel under the delicate glory of the lilac trees.

Manchester Square basked in this morning oasis of tranquility and there was no other place so quiet or so well ordered as the tall, thin house belonging to Lady Amelia Godolphin.

Straight, thin columns of smoke rose up into the sky, and a thin, red line of tulips guarded the window boxes.

Then scream after shocking scream of rage and anguish rent the peace, rising from Lady Amelia Godolphin's mansion in an ever increasing crescendo. Startled pigeons soared away from the roofs and bustled about the sky, faces appeared like small moons behind lacy clouds of twitching curtains at the surrounding windows. The screams went on. Doors popped open. A crowd began to gather in that mysterious way of crowds. One minute the square was empty, the next a bunch of people appeared to have sprouted from the pavement.

The blinds of Lady Amelia's house were hurriedly drawn, a liveried footman bounded up the area steps followed by two small boys and started directing them to lay straw on the pavement and on the road to muffle the sounds of any passing wheels, and still the terrible screams went on and on.

The crowd at first was convinced that someone was being murdered in the politest manner possible but, all too soon, it had the truth of the matter.

Bad news travels posthaste. As the last scream died away, the news had spread like wildfire through the West End.

London's reigning beauty, London's richest woman, my Lady Amelia Godolphin had been refused a voucher to Almack's.

Almack's Assembly Rooms were the seventh heaven of the fashionable world. Balls were held during the Season on Wednesday nights and tremendous importance was attached to getting vouchers of admission to this exclusive temple of the *beau monde*.

The lady patronesses were the Ladies Castlereigh, Jersey, Cowper and Sefton, Mrs Drummond Burrell, the Princess Esterhazy, and Countess Lieven.

Almack's popularity was the result of a wave of snobbery which was sweeping London. There was no point, after all, in belonging to the *ton* if you could not get somewhere that was banned to lesser mortals. These dances had introduced something new into English life: a rigid, narrow and inhuman pride. The most vulgar and despotic of the patronesses — and therefore the most snobbish — was that haughty and indefatigable beauty, Lady Jersey. These rooms she reigned over had also become the highest marriage market in Britain where some of the richest bachelors in the world could be seen executing Scottish reels to the fiddling of Neil Gow's band.

Hence Lady Amelia Godolphin's screaming despair. For Lady Amelia not only wished to remarry and marry well, but she had already set her sights as high as Lord Philip Cautry, a handsome and moneyed aristocrat whose line dated back to the mists of antiquity.

Lady Amelia was beautiful and very rich. She was the daughter of an impoverished Irish peer who had shocked London by marrying a wealthy and elderly Cit, Harold Godolphin, at the end of her first Season. That she had married the rich businessman for his money was never in doubt and he obliged her by dying some six months after the wedding and leaving her his immense fortune.

Amelia had gladly taken the money and had set out to kick up her heels around the Town. At first her exploits were more hoydenish than scandalous, but she ended up having a much publicized affair with the middle-aged Duke of Glendurran, despite the noisy objections of the Duchess. Just when it seemed as if the Duke might divorce his wife in order to marry Amelia, he died of a heart attack, brought on, said Society maliciously, by his constant and strenuous efforts to behave like a much younger man to charm his fair mistress.

Lady Amelia had promptly rusticated in Italy for two years and then, assuming that the polite world would have forgotten her affair, she had returned to London to prepare for a Season and to woo Lord Philip.

As she was very rich, titled, young, and beautiful, all doors were open to her but that all-important one — Almack's. Lord Philip Cautry was known to be notoriously high in the instep and would not take a wife who was not socially acceptable everywhere.

At last her screams subsided into noisy sobbing and her lady's maid knew, from long experience, that it was now safe to start to quietly clean up the damage of shattered china and to arrange for the looking glass to be repaired yet again.

Lady Amelia dried her blue eyes on a corner of the sheet and straightened her nightcap with hands which still trembled with rage and disappointment. She wrenched herself from the bed and stormed to a small writing desk in the corner and began to scribble busily. Then she held out the finished letter to the lady's maid, Eliot.

'Eliot, see that a footman takes this round to Mrs Besant *immediately*,' she demanded and, as Eliot scurried from the room, she sat tapping her foot and staring stormily into space.

An odd sort of friendship had developed long ago between the young and beautiful Amelia and the middle-aged and waspish Mrs Mary Besant. Perhaps it was simply because the pair delighted in rending apart the characters of their friends and acquaintances. Mrs Besant was also a widow and her sour appearance and sharp tongue ensured that she would always remain so, having nagged her meek husband into an early grave. Lady Amelia, unlike her friend, had the sense to try to curb her tongue in public and although — all too often — her flashes of malice would dart forth, she was, in the main, readily forgiven because of her beauty.

She had pale blue eyes like a spring sky, hair so fair that it was nearly white, and a tall, willowy figure.

She hoped Mrs Besant would reply to her summons and come immediately. She rang the bell for Eliot and stood like a beautiful statue while the lady's maid dressed her in a pale blue redingote, the colour of her eyes.

Amelia was just descending the stairs when Mrs Besant was announced and both women walked together into the rose saloon.

Mrs Besant was dressed in an unbecoming puce walking dress of almost mannish severity. She had a thin, rouged face with a high-bridged nose and large yellowing teeth. Her thin lips were parted in her customary smile which never seemed to reach her pale grey eyes.

Society was thoroughly frightened of her and therefore considered her good *ton*, although, before she married the late Mr Besant who hailed from the untitled aristocracy, Mrs Besant had been a vicar's daughter. A few bold sparks had tried from time to time to snub the formidable widow, but she had immediately retaliated by finding out something unsavoury or embarrassing about each of her tormentors and had duly broadcast it in the sweetest way imaginable.

'Well, Amelia?' she began. 'I trust it is something important. I have not yet had my chocolate.'

'Of *course* it's important,' snapped Amelia. 'I am not in the habit of hailing you from your bed at dawn.' It was eleven o'clock, but then that *was* dawn to a fashionable Londoner. 'I have been refused vouchers to Almack's!'

'Disaster. Absolute and utter disaster,' breathed Mrs Besant, enjoying the mortification of her pretty friend immensely. 'Sally Jersey, I suppose.'

'Chattering idiot,' said Amelia venomously, meaning Lady Jersey. 'How on earth that vulgar woman came to have such social power, I will never know. What will Cautry think of it? He is warm in his attentions, but I mean to be Lady Cautry and not his mistress.'

Mrs Besant privately thought that Lord Philip Cautry would not be swayed by the dictates of Almack's were his affections fixed, but that might have eased the anguish of Lady Amelia and Mrs Besant thrived on other people's distress.

'It is indeed a problem, Amelia,' said Mrs Besant with scarcely veiled satisfaction. 'It was your affair with Glendurran, you know. I always said . . .'

'Oh, stow it,' said Lady Amelia who never wasted her breath trying to be polite to Mrs Besant. 'Don't tell me what I ought not to have done. Tell me what I am to do!'

Mrs Besant pursed her thin lips. 'You need to become respectable, Amelia,' she said at last. 'Do you think I could have a taste of wine to moisten my lips? You know I don't drink in the ordinary way but this is, after all, a special occasion. Thank you. Now, where was I? Ah, yes. Respectability.

'You see, my dear,' she went on, moistening her lips with large gulps of madeira, 'what you really need is someone to live with you. Some female of irreproachable character, the churchier the better. Gentlemen pay calls on you, you see, and it is known that you are unchaperoned. Now, could Society see you everywhere with some stern dragon of a companion, they would soon change their minds.'

'Who do you suggest?' said Amelia, narrowing her eyes. 'Yourself?'

'Dear me, no!' exclaimed Mrs Besant. 'I am a wealthy woman and much too much good *ton* to be a companion to anyone. Put an advertisement in the newspapers.

'And now I must rush. I am attending a breakfast at the Cholmleys'. I shall see you there, of course.'

'Of course,' said Amelia with a bright smile. She had not been invited and was burning again with rage and humiliation, but was determined not to let Mrs Besant see her distress.

But Mrs Besant noticed the clenching fingers and took her leave in high good humour. For she, Mrs Besant, had not, of course, been invited to the Cholmleys' breakfast. Nor for that matter were the Cholmleys even giving a breakfast. But when your friends were down, it really was a source of satisfaction if you could make sure they stayed there.

Amelia said a very unladylike word as soon as Mrs Besant was out of earshot. First Almack's and now the Cholmleys. It was too much!

But the old harridan had certainly produced a good idea. A companion would be the answer. But who?

I must have a poor relation somewhere, thought Amelia, her busy mind running back and forth along the branches of her family tree. A relation would not cost much. A relation would be more under her thumb than some paid professional. A relation would do it in return for bed and board and would not need wages. The Irish branch of the family would not do. The Irish could be very independent. Her mother had been English. Perhaps someone on that side of the family . . .

Then she gave a slow smile. She had suddenly hit on just the person. There was a cousin of her late mother, a Miss Maria Lamberton, of irreproachable lineage and terrifying morals. Amelia remembered the grim spinster from her childhood, a thin, upright old lady, forever quoting the Bible and with not a penny to her name. Miss Lamberton could moralize all she liked in public but she, Amelia, would make sure she knew her place and kept her tongue still in private.

She began to search through her papers, looking for the address. Ah, here it was. Miss Lamberton, Berry House, Witherton, Essex. Miss Lamberton it should be. How could Society think ill of her with such a companion by her side? She remembered her mother saying that Berry House was little more than a cottage with a few straggling acres, and mortgaged up to the hilt.

She sat down and began to write busily.

'My dear Miss Lamberton . . .'

Chapter Two

Miss Lamberton put down Lady Amelia's letter after reading it for the third time and stared out across the unkempt lawn of Berry House where a few scrawny hens were searching for worms.

An incessant drizzle fell across the scraggly garden, soaking into the spongy ground and moss-covered trees. Everything was soaked in moisture, the hearths in the house were black and empty and new damp patches had added their stains to the old brown ones on the walls.

Miss Constance Lamberton picked up the letter again. Her aunt, Miss Maria Lamberton, for whom the letter was obviously intended although it was merely addressed to 'Miss Lamberton,' lay six feet under the wet clay soil of the local churchyard where she had been deposited a week before.

For one precious minute Constance had thought the letter an answer to all her troubles. Her aunt had left no will, so after a long and legal hassle the heavily mortgaged house with its bleak grounds and worm-eaten furniture would go to a distant male relative. Constance had already been searching the newspapers for a position as governess. She had sent off three applications but, so far, had received no replies.

She turned her attention to the letter again. 'You would be furnished with all the comforts of an elegant home and all the enjoyment of the balls and parties of the Season,' Lady Amelia had written. 'All I ask in return is that you accept the post as my companion. I am sure we should suit admirably . . .'

A Season! Constance clasped her hands, crumpling the letter in the process. She had not dreamt of a Season since her twelfth birthday. She had been brought up in a haphazard manner by her wild and feckless father, Sir Edward Lamberton. Her mother had died of consumption when Constance was only a baby. She had adored her boyish father, had been petted and fussed over by his sporting friends, and had enjoyed when their shabby home, Courtleigh, had been full of male guests who would descend on them *en masse* for a long session of hunting and gambling. But Sir Edward had broken his neck on the hunting field, leaving his daughter nothing but a vast pile of debts, and sad memories of the glittering Season her father had promised her she should have when she came of age.

His sister, Maria Lamberton, had appeared at the funeral and announced it to be her Christian duty to care for the orphaned Constance. She had taken the girl back to Berry House and had proceeded to subject Constance to a rigorous religious training. Miss Lamberton felt she had snatched a brand from the burning. No more pretty dresses and jewellery for young Constance. Only dowdy alpacas and serge to be worn while she passed her leisure time reading the only two books allowed to her — the Bible and Mr Porteous's sermons.

Miss Maria had been considerably older than her wild brother and had died of one of these mysterious ailments of old age.

Now, a week after her death, Constance was again left homeless. It seemed that Miss Lamberton had been, in her way, as much of a gambler as her brother, always spending money on wild farming ventures in the hope that her meagre acres would produce a fortune, but instead, every blight and animal

20

pest seemed to find a home at Berry House. Miss Lamberton had also been so preoccupied in preparing herself and Constance for the afterlife that it had never dawned on her that she might reach that happy place sooner than she expected, and so she had not troubled to make a will.

Berry House was quite isolated, the nearest village being some ten miles away. Miss Lamberton had had few callers. Although she said her thoughts were constantly in heaven, her speech dwelled only too often on the tortures of hellfire, and even the vicar called as infrequently as possible. The house was, indeed, as small as Lady Amelia had heard it to be, being a sort of redbrick box with small, dark rooms. It had been many years since Miss Lamberton had had any servants, and such work as there was was done by herself and Constance.

When her father had died, Constance had been a merry, happy little twelve-year-old. Now, on the eve of her eighteenth birthday she was still very small but thin and bony. Her hands were deformed and scarred with the winter's crop of chilblains and her skin was stretched tight over her high cheekbones. Her black hair was screwed up in a knot on the top of her small head and was greasy and dirty, Miss Lamberton having

21

considered that cleanliness was an over preoccupation with vanity, rather than being next to godliness. Constance was very small in stature, being a mere five feet, two inches. The only thing that lent any colour to her otherwise drab appearance was a pair of large and unusually beautiful eyes which were of a light, golden brown flecked with gold and fringed with heavy black lashes.

Under the influence of her aunt, she had almost come to believe that dreams of balls and parties were sinful. But now, without the overbearing presence of her aunt, her imagination seemed to have run riot.

As she sat holding Lady Amelia's letter, she could almost *see* the ballroom of her dreams and smell the scent from the expensively gowned ladies. And if she closed her eyes very tightly, she could feel *his* arms about her, that forbidden dream lover, that young man with the boyish face and curly hair who had long haunted her thoughts. She had never actually seen such a man but over the years she had invented one — a man who would be the perfect companion and husband. Someone to laugh and have fun with. Someone gay and debonair who would stand between her and the rest of the forbidding world which stretched beyond Berry House.

What else had Lady Amelia said in her letter? 'I want some respectable lady of good birth to be my chaperone.'

'Why couldn't it be me?' thought Constance. 'I'm a respectable lady of good birth!'

It was then that a mad idea, born of insecurity and despair, began to take shape in her mind.

The letter had been addressed to Miss Lamberton. 'I am Miss Lamberton,' thought Constance. 'Could I not just go to London and apply for the post? I am, after all, a relative of Lady Amelia. Surely she would not turn me away if I explain the situation.'

The evening sky was turning black outside and a faint wind had begun to moan — through the trees. Constance lit the foul-smelling tallow candles and went to look into the flyblown looking glass over the fireplace.

Her thin, white face stared back at her, the eyes looking enormous in the flickering gloom. 'You haven't *said* you'll do it,' she muttered. 'But at least you could wash your hair.'

With quick nervous steps, she descended to the kitchen and then began to pile wood into the fire. When the flames began to leap up, she hung the great kettle on the idle back, a long sort of hook with an ingenious contrivance by which it could be tipped to pour out boiling water.

Then taking a sharp knife, she shaved fine pieces from a bar of soap into a cup, and adding a little water, mashed them into a paste. When the kettle began to boil, she first infused a jug of camomile tea and let it stand to cool so that she could use it for a rinse.

She washed and washed her hair until her arms ached. Then she took down the tin bath from its hook on the wall and waited for more water to heat.

By the time she had bathed, she decided to indulge in the extravagance of washing her clothes. Clothes at Berry House had only been washed every five weeks, in the same way as the laundry was done in almost every other genteel house in England.

After two hours of hard work, she stood shivering in her wrapper in her bedroom, staring at the glossy tresses of black hair which fell almost to her waist.

'I shall keep my hair like this, just for tonight and all of tomorrow morning. Then when I travel to London, I must make myself look as old and staid as possible.'

Constance nearly dropped the hairbrush

as she realized that somehow she *was* going to London.

Her mind began to race. There was the house to close up. She would need to leave the keys with the vicar, ready for the arrival of Aunt Maria's heir who, it was believed, lived somewhere in Hertfordshire.

Constance suddenly wondered if she were being too precipitate. Might it not be better to remain where she was and rely on the charity of the heir?

But the lure of London was strong. She had an overwhelming desire to escape from this dark house with its grim memories of harsh religious training. She wished to flee from an overpowering feeling of guilt caused by the fact she could not mourn for the dead Miss Lamberton.

As she brushed and brushed her long black hair, the great shining toy of the London Season beckoned.

She put down the brush and knelt at her prayer stool through force of habit. But this time she found herself praying for security, for love and for a home of her own.

Constance finally arose and climbed into bed with the feeling she had left her childhood with all its miseries behind.

'Travelling post,' she thought dreamily as she watched the patterns thrown by the

rushlight on the ceiling, 'is too expensive —
eighteen pence a mile. But there is enough
left from the year's sale of eggs to pay for a
seat on the mail coach. I wonder if the egg
money really belongs to the heir? If it does,
I shall just have to pay him back when I am
a rich and married lady.'

And lulled by rosy dreams of security,
Constance fell sound asleep.

Chapter Three

Lady Amelia's butler did not look like a butler at all. Friends of her ladyship were wont to murmur behind her back that her butler, Bergen, looked more like a jailbird. Butlers were meant to be quiet, discreet individuals, but there was something about Bergen that was *too* quiet. Where other butlers moved with a slow and stately tread, Bergen scuttled softly from room to room with an odd, bent, crablike walk. His long, lugubrious face was also tilted to one side, giving him an air of constant enquiry. His bony wrists protruded from the sleeves of his uniform, and his hair was never sufficiently powdered and black patches always seemed to be showing through.

Mrs Mary Besant eyed this individual with disfavour as she entered the hall of Lady Amelia's mansion late one afternoon, a full two weeks after her previous visit. Her sharp eyes fell on the morning's post, still lying unopened on the marble top of a pretty mahogany side table.

'I see her ladyship has not yet perused her mail,' she said to Bergen. 'I shall take it up to her.'

'My lady said she had no time to read her mail at present,' said Bergen, with his head tilted to one side like a raven at the Tower.

'Nonetheless, I shall take it up to her,' said Mrs Besant, gathering up the little pile of letters and cards. She stood and stared coldly at the butler. 'That will be all, Bergen.'

'I shall announce you, madam,' said the infuriating Bergen, staring at the correspondence in Mrs Besant's pink-gloved hands.

Mrs Besant had no intention of letting Bergen announce her. In the first place, she delighted in surprising her friends at their toilette. Had she not, just the other day, discovered that Lady Jessington wore a wig by just such a ruse? In the second, she planned to extract one or two of the invitations and hide them in her reticule so that dear Amelia would smart with humiliation, thinking she had been slighted.

'I shall announce myself,' she said waspishly. 'Bustle about, man. I am sure you have other duties.'

Bergen gave her a low bow and retreated. Mrs Besant walked up the wide shallow stairs and gleefully flicked through the letters. Ah, she recognized that seal. Lord Philip Cautry's sister, Lady Eleanor Rider, was giving a *musicale*, that much she knew, having received an invitation herself. How furious Amelia would be if she thought she had been excluded from the guest list! Quick as lightning, Mrs Besant slipped the invitation in her reticule, and feeling very pleased with herself, walked into Lady Amelia's private sitting-room.

To her disappointment, Amelia was fully dressed and looking more beautiful than ever.

'I brought your post, my dear,' said Mrs Besant with a great display of strong, yellow teeth. 'Don't you want to see if you have received any billets-doux?'

'I probably have,' said Amelia, stretching out her hand for the letters. 'That wretched Comte Duval is always writing some sort of rubbish to me!'

'Many ladies would be delighted to receive such letters from the comte!' exclaimed Mrs Besant. The Comte Duval was a rare bird among the French emigrés who haunted London. Unlike most of his compatriots, he was extremely rich.

Amelia paid her no attention. She scrabbled through the letters and invitations, a small frown beginning to crease her beautiful brow. 'I had thought the Riders' invitation would have arrived by now,' she said.

Mrs Besant gave a little titter. 'Oh, poor Amelia, I have had my own invitation for *ages*. Never say the Cautry family has turned against you!'

She watched in delight as the storm clouds began to gather in Amelia's blue eyes, and then jumped nervously as a hollow cough sounded directly behind her. She swung round and found herself looking into the pale gooseberry eyes of Bergen, the butler.

'My lady,' he began, 'there is a young person waiting below to see you. A Miss Lamberton. I have put her in the library.'

'A *young* person? You must be mistaken, Bergen. Miss Lamberton is old.'

'No, my lady. Definitely young,' said Bergen.

Amelia stared at him for a few minutes and then shrugged. 'Well, whoever this Miss Lamberton is, I had better see her. Oh, and Bergen, could you check carefully in the hall and make sure that *all* my post has been delivered to me? I am missing a most important invitation.'

'Perhaps it is the one that madam put into her reticule — for safekeeping I am sure,' said Bergen, his head on one side, looking carefully at the floor.

'What is this?' cried Amelia.

'I-I don't know what he is talking about,' said Mrs Besant turning an unlovely shade of puce. 'My good man, are you accusing me of stealing my lady's correspondence? Why, I . . .'

But that was as far as she got. Amelia wrenched the reticule from Mrs Besant's shaking fingers and tore it open. She pulled out the Rider invitation and waved it to and fro slowly in front of Mrs Besant's patrician nose.

'Think of some excuse, dear Mary,' she said softly, 'I shall be back as soon as I have seen this Lamberton woman.'

Amelia left the room in high good humour. The idea of making Mary Besant sweat a little was exhilarating. Old cat!

She tripped lightly into the library and stared in amazement at the young female who was rising to her feet to meet her.

Amelia saw a very thin, young girl with a pinched white face dressed in a brown wool gown, much patched and mended, and wearing, as she afterwards said, 'The worst quiz of a bonnet I ever did see.'

'You are not the Miss Lamberton I wrote to. Who are you?' demanded Amelia.

'An it please your ladyship,' said the girl in a low voice, 'I *am* Miss Lamberton. Miss Constance Lamberton. My aunt passed away, you see, but I thought . . . I hoped . . . th-that you would perhaps employ me as your companion instead,' she ended in a breathless rush.

'Good heavens, no,' said Amelia crossly. 'You are much too young to play chaperone. Of course I wouldn't dream of hiring you. Be off with you!'

'But — but I have nowhere to go tonight,' wailed Constance in despair. 'Could I at least wait until morning?'

'No, of course not. Go away!' said Amelia petulantly.

'Is there anything I can do to help?' came the sugary voice of Mrs Besant from the doorway.

'No!' snapped Amelia. 'This chit is nothing but an imposter. Old Maria's dead, and this person claims to be her niece.'

Constance raised her magnificent eyes hopefully to Mrs Besant's face and then dropped them hurriedly. She saw no signs of a champion there.

But in that she was wrong.

Amelia had been yawning fretfully and

staring at the wall, but Mary Besant had caught the full impact of those beautiful eyes. If Constance Lamberton were well-fed and well-clothed, why, she might be quite a beauty, thought Mrs Besant, and wouldn't Amelia just *hate* that!

'Amelia, my love, a word with you in private. 'Tis *most* important!'

'Oh, very well,' said Amelia with a gleam of interest in her eye. She was longing to know how Mary Besant meant to worm her way out of her crime of stealing. 'You may go,' she said to Constance.

But as Constance was trailing dejectedly from the room, Mary Besant whispered urgently. 'No, keep her for the moment until you hear what I have to say. You, Miss Lamberton,' she said in a louder voice, 'are you Sir Edward Lamberton's gel?'

'Yes, ma'am,' said Constance in a pathetic voice which broke on a sob.

'As I thought,' smiled Mrs Besant. 'Wait in the hall a moment.'

Constance stared wildly at Lady Amelia with sudden hope. But then her face fell. Lady Amelia was examining her own beautiful face in the looking glass as if Miss Lamberton had never existed.

Mrs Besant waited until the double doors had closed behind the shabby figure of

Constance and then turned eagerly to her friend.

'Now, before I begin, Amelia,' she said eagerly, 'you know that diamond pendant you so admired the other day?'

'Yes,' said Amelia slowly, a pale light of avarice beginning to dawn in her eyes.

'Well, it is yours, my dear — to make up for my stupid lapse of memory in taking your invitation by mistake.'

Amelia looked at Mary Besant thoughtfully and tapped her small foot. 'There is a very fine pair of earrings that go with it,' she said softly.

Mary Besant's eyes widened. Bloodsucker! Amelia had all the grasping greed of a Haymarket Cyprian. But if she, Mary, did not pay up then, by tomorrow morning all the world and his wife would know that she had purloined that letter!

'But of course, how remiss of me,' she said with a painful smile. 'Of course, the earrings as well.'

'Very well,' said Amelia with an expression on her face like that of a well-fed cat. 'Now, tell me, what is all this about that depressing Lamberton female? La! What a quiz.'

'That,' said Mrs Besant dramatically pointing in the direction of the hall. 'That is the way to Philip Cautry's heart.'

'Fustian!' said Amelia roundly. 'That drab!'

'But listen, my dear. Only listen. Sir Edward Lamberton was a wastrel and a rake-hell, but very well beloved by Society and very, very good *ton. And he taught Lord Philip Cautry to hunt!* For you know Lord Philip's papa was a scholar and did not care for sports. 'Tis said Lord Philip was devoted to Sir Edward when he, Philip, was a boy. In fact, he once was heard to wonder what had become of the little Lamberton girl. Now, if *you* were to give such a respectable — such a *dull* little girl a home. Think on't! Philip would smile on you, would he not? Society would consider you had done more than your duty in rescuing one of their kind from poverty. Also,' added Mrs Besant cleverly, ' 'twould be a marvellous foil for you! The girl is so plain and quiet. How she would set off your beauty!'

'Have her in again!' said Amelia abruptly.

Mrs Besant threw open the doors triumphantly and called Constance.

Both women walked around the drab figure of Miss Lamberton, Mrs Besant praying that the girl would keep those eyes *down*.

'Yes,' said Amelia slowly. 'Very clever, Mary. Very clever indeed. I am beholden to you. Well, Constance, I have decided to give you the post.' Those magnificent eyes flashed up, but Lady Amelia was too preoccupied with her scheme to notice. 'You will receive your bed and board, but no more. You will go about with me in Society and you will tell anyone who asks that it is thanks to my condescension that you have a home. Do you understand?'

'Oh, yes,' breathed Constance.

'You will need to be suitably dressed as befits my companion,' went on Lady Amelia thoughtfully. 'Something plain and neat. Grey silk, I think . . .'

But Mary Besant had another brainwave. 'My dear Amelia,' she cried. 'Only think of the needless expense! And you have so many gowns you will never wear again.'

'That's very true,' said Amelia, the idea appealing immensely to her cheese-paring nature. 'Eliot, my maid, shall find you something suitable.'

Mrs Besant sighed with satisfaction. Better that Miss Lamberton should be attired in Amelia's gorgeous castoffs than in the drab colours that Amelia would undoubtedly have chosen for her.

Amelia touched the bell. 'Ah, Bergen,' she said when the butler scuttled in. 'Miss Lamberton is staying. She is my new companion. Take her things up and show her to some room or other.'

Constance was hardly able to believe her good fortune as she followed the butler up the stairs. She could not understand why such a hard-faced woman as Mrs Besant had interceded on her behalf, but she was too grateful to have a roof over her head.

Bergen led the way on up and up until he reached a region of low ceilings and uncarpeted corridors. He pushed open a low door and dumped Constance's bandbox on the bare floor of a small attic room which was unfurnished except for a narrow iron bedstead and one hard chair.

'This is yours,' he said with a pale glint of malice in his eyes. But then it was his turn to jump as Mary Besant's voice grated in his ear. 'No, no, Bergen. You must have taken leave of your senses. This will not do. Not at all. Miss Lamberton is not a servant, like you. Find something suitable for a lady of quality. I am sure we shall be friends,' she said to Constance but with her eyes on the butler. 'I never forget my friends — or my enemies for that matter, heh, Bergen?'

Bergen gave her a surly look but led the way down the stairs again to a more luxurious region. He pushed open a door. Mrs Besant took a quick look round. 'This will do very nicely, Bergen. That will be all. You may go — as far away as possible.'

Bergen slouched off and Constance looked about her in amazement. A charming sitting-room with walls panelled in delicate green silk led to a spacious bedroom with a large four-poster bed. The furniture was light and delicate and the curtains and carpets glowed with colour. A small fire crackled briskly on the hearth.

'This cannot be for me!' she exclaimed.

'But it is. Of course it is,' said Mrs Besant, putting an arm around the girl and pressing a bony hip uncomfortably into her side. 'Just remember always that you have Mary Besant to thank for it.'

'How can I ever repay you?' cried Constance.

'Don't worry,' murmured Mary Besant, baring her teeth and giving the girl another hard squeeze. 'You'll think of something.'

She gave a terrible horse-laugh and Constance laughed with her, although she could not see what there was that was so funny.

When Mary Besant had left after a final bony squeeze, Constance was further surprised by the arrival of a small maid bearing a tray with a cold supper laid out on it. The maid bobbed a curtsy and said, 'My lady says you are to rest tonight, miss, and to start your duties tomorrow.'

'Thank you,' murmured Constance gratefully. Lady Amelia was kind after all!

'I am very, very lucky,' thought Constance when she was left alone with her supper. 'I must do my best to repay all this by being the best companion ever. And I shall start by praying for the Lady Amelia . . . and Mrs Besant.'

She got down on her knees on the pretty carpet and prayed dutifully for Lady Amelia, a gesture which would have caused that young lady considerable mirth if she could have known.

Chapter Four

Lady Eleanor Rider took another complacent look at the arrangements for her *musicale*. Rout chairs were neatly lined in rows in the blue salon where a small dais holding a pianoforte and several palms had been erected at one end. The refreshments had been arranged in an adjoining salon, and footmen were putting final touches to elaborate banks of hothouse flowers which lined the walls.

Everyone who was anyone would be there that evening, for Lady Eleanor prided herself on her entertainments and was ever-conscious of her ancient family name. It was a pity, she reflected, that she could not have married a title instead of plain Mr George Rider who, although blue-blooded, unfortunately hailed from the untitled aristocracy. She only hoped that her brother Philip would honour his promise and put in an appearance.

Her complacent eye ran once more over the guest list and then widened as the name Lady Amelia Godolphin seemed to leap out of the page. She rang the bell and asked the butler to fetch Mr Rider's secretary *immediately*.

A thin, young man with sandy hair and a nervous tic quickly answered her summons. 'Mr Evans,' demanded Lady Eleanor imperiously, 'pray explain what Lady Amelia Godolphin's name is doing on my guest list.'

Mr Evans' worried expression cleared. 'That was Mr Rider's suggestion, madam,' he said. 'Mr Rider was entertaining the Comte Duval and Monsieur le Comte mentioned that he was looking forward to the *musicale* and said he hoped to see Lady Amelia there and Mr Rider said of course she would be, and asked me to make a note of it.'

'Blast the man!' muttered Lady Eleanor in a way that boded ill for her absent spouse. 'I am most displeased, Mr Evans. I invite only the highest of the *ton* to this house and I do not consider that female good *ton*. Make a note of that! She is *never* to be invited here again.'

'Very good, madam,' said Mr Evans woodenly.

'And if you are doing nothing else at the moment, you can check the arrangements. See that Mr Favioli's music is properly arranged.' Mr Favioli was the male soprano who was to entertain the company that evening.

'I have letters for Mr Rider . . .' began the secretary, his voice trailing away under Lady Eleanor's steely glare. 'But you have time to help,' finished Lady Eleanor for him. Mr Evans walked off to attend to the music, and Lady Eleanor walked briskly to the hall as she heard the sounds of her husband's arrival.

Lady Eleanor was a tall, harsh-faced woman with a well-upholstered figure, severe black hair and a cold black eye. By contrast, Mr Rider was a small, fussy, timid man, and it was said that Lady Eleanor had borne him off to the altar, rather than the other way around. The couple was childless, and since they were both now in their middle years, the wags had given up pointing out that Lady Eleanor's commanding stare was enough to turn the veriest Don Juan impotent.

'What is this nonsense about inviting Amelia Godolphin?' she demanded, without waiting for him to remove his hat.

'Who?' said her husband blinking rapidly.

'I'm very sorry, my dear,' he added, apologizing quickly and meekly with the air of a man who has spent his life apologizing for one thing or the other.

'So you should be,' she snapped. 'But you men are all the same. Carried away by the sight of a pretty ankle. You'll be inviting tavern wenches next, that you will.'

'My dear, I assure . . .'

'But then, you always had a bold eye for the ladies,' remarked Lady Eleanor. Her husband's eye blinked at her as boldly as a startled rabbit's, but he was too used to his wife accusing him of being a ladies' man to take her remark very seriously.

'Come into the drawing-room,' went on Lady Eleanor. 'I wish to talk to you about Philip.'

Mr Rider followed her meekly. 'Sit down,' said Lady Eleanor. 'Now, Philip has just celebrated his thirty-second year and it is time he was thinking of settling down. It is time we introduced him to a suitable girl.'

'Quite, my dear,' said her husband faintly.

'Now, there is a young lady, a Miss Limrighton, who will be here tonight. She is just the sort of girl Philip should marry. I want you to make sure that they are introduced to each other. Also, think up some ruse to get them left alone together.'

Mr Rider thought of his toplofty, arrogant brother-in-law who, if the rumours were to be believed, had already a very pretty lady-bird in keeping.

'Well, you know,' he said timidly, 'Philip will not listen to me, and surely you could arrange it better.'

'Nonsense!' said his wife. 'These sort of things are better handled by a man. Too pushing in a lady of my breeding. You will do it, that is all, and we shall have a comfortable coze about it after the evening is over.'

Mr Rider's heart sank. His wife's idea of a comfortable coze was to interrogate him of his doings of the day, and then tell him in her forceful manner where he had gone wrong.

But, 'Just as you say,' he bleated, and began to edge out of the room in search of his secretary.

He ran Mr Evans to earth behind the platform in the blue salon. Both Mr Rider and his secretary were weak and timorous men and found much solace in each other's company. Mr Rider gloomily outlined his duties for the evening, and for once found to his amazement that his secretary was prepared to take the burden from his shoulders.

'Lord Philip Cautry has been very kind to me,' said Mr Evans, 'and has, in fact, signalled me out from time to time in order to ask me kindly how I go on. I am not afraid of him,' said Mr Evans puffing out his thin chest, 'and I would be happy to do this service for you, sir.'

Mr Rider looked at his secretary with dawning admiration. 'But how will you get him to step aside with the sort of young female that my wife considers suitable?' he asked.

'I shall tell him I have been commanded to do so,' said Mr Evans. 'He will be annoyed but he will do it to oblige me.'

Mr Rider eyed Mr Evans doubtfully. 'Very well then, Evans. I hear the carriages beginning to arrive. Do your best, man. But don't blame me if Cautry gives you one of his set downs!'

Constance looked out at the flickering lights of London as Lady Amelia's carriage picked its way through the West End. She felt very tired and very apprehensive. She had come to dread Amelia's fickle and malicious humours. A week had passed since her arrival in Manchester Square, and already her duties seemed to be more burdensome than that of an overworked lady's maid. She had to dance constant attendance on Amelia, who treated her with sugary sweetness in public and mocked her in private. Amelia delighted in shocking her well-bred companion, and there were many of the more sordid facts of life dinned into Constance's red ears. Amelia had also found that her companion was an expert needlewoman; and noticing how skilfully the companion had altered certain dresses of Amelia's for her own use, Amelia had plunged into an orgy of material buying, and poor Constance seemed to spend all her spare time sewing and stitching.

Constance enjoyed the visits to the theatre or the opera the best, for in the darkness at the back of the box, she found she could catch up on some much needed sleep. The servants were frightened of Mrs Besant and therefore treated the new companion with wary respect. She was elegantly dressed and well-fed for the first time since the death of her father, but she would gladly have changed it all for the strict rule of Maria Lamberton. On each social occasion, she had to suffer Amelia's patronizing intro-ductions, 'Oh, this is a poor little relative of mine — old Edward Lamberton's girl, you know — I couldn't let her *starve,* my dears.'

Constance had also come to dread the presence of the Comte Duval who would pay court to Amelia, while all the while his

46

snapping black eyes would watch Constance like a cat watching a mouse. Amelia encouraged the comte shamelessly to bolder gallantries, enjoying Constance's very obvious discomfort.

One evening after the opera, it almost seemed as if the comte would stay the night, but Amelia had at last stopped his lovemaking and had said with a light laugh, 'You must go, my dear Pierre. I am become respectable, you see, and plan to marry soon,' and then had laughed at the comte's startled face. 'Not you, stupid. I plan to wed Cautry.'

'Cautry!' Duval had sneered. 'He will never have you!'

'Oh, but he will,' Amelia had mocked, her eyes swivelling to look at Constance who was sitting looking as uncomfortable as a gooseberry usually feels. 'I have a plan, you see . . .'

Constance now wondered just what that plan was. She knew that Amelia planned to meet Philip Cautry that very evening. Amelia had dressed with great care for the occasion in a dress of spider gauze held with diamond clasps over an underdress of palest pink silk. The diamond pendant from Mrs Besant burned at her throat and long diamond drops ornamented her tiny ears. She wore a magnificently fairy-tale tiara atop her heavy fair hair. Constance privately thought her mistress a trifle over-dressed for such an occasion, but Amelia seemed thoroughly pleased with the dazzling picture she presented. Constance was demurely dressed in an old rose silk gown of Amelia's, which had pretty puffed sleeves and three deep vandyked flounces at the hem.

Her only ornament was a seed pearl necklace belonging to her late mother, and her thick black hair was braided in a coronet on top of her small head. Regular feeding had added some much needed flesh to her slight form and, had Amelia not been so ridiculously vain, she would have noticed that her companion was becoming unsuitably pretty. But Mrs Besant had noticed, and had rubbed her hands in glee. Constance's wellbred air made Amelia appear rather overblown and showy by contrast, and Mrs Besant did so hope that Lord Philip Cautry would notice that contrast.

The carriage drew up at last in front of a very elegant mansion in Berkeley Square.

Lady Eleanor stood at the top of the steps leading to the blue salon and watched Amelia moving up the red-carpeted stairs towards her. She gave the infuriated Amelia a mere two fingers to shake and then turned her frosty glare on the figure of Constance.

'And who is this?' she demanded.

'My companion, Miss Lamberton,' murmured Amelia. 'You know, old Edward Lamberton's girl. Absolutely starving and no home of her own. I had to take her in. It was the least I could do.'

'Indeed!' Lady Eleanor glared awfully at Constance who blushed miserably and wondered what she had done to offend. She did not know that Lady Eleanor blamed Sir Edward Lamberton for introducing her young brother, Philip, to all the wild and rakish sports that she so much deplored.

'Indeed!' she said again. 'Then I am afraid Miss . . . er . . . Lamberton will need to wait in some anteroom. I was not expecting you to bring anyone, Lady Godolphin, and I only have space in the salon for the guests who were *invited*.'

'Oh, very well,' shrugged Amelia. 'Put her where you will.' And without turning to see whether anyone was taking care of Constance, she sailed on into the blue salon.

Lady Eleanor half turned and summoned Mr Evans with an imperious wave of her hand. 'Ah, Mr Evans, this is Miss Lamberton. We do not have a chair for her at the *musicale,* so please put her in some room to wait until the entertainment is over.'

'Very good, madam,' beamed Mr Evans. He thought Lady Eleanor had said 'Miss Limrighton,' and that Lady Eleanor was helping with the plot. He would put her in the library and send Lord Philip to her!

Constance, who had been feeling miserable over the coldness of her reception, brightened considerably under Mr Evans's care. At least here was someone who seemed absolutely delighted to see her. He ushered her into the library, rang for a footman, and demanded that a selection of the *best* of the supper be brought in along with a bottle of champagne.

'I shall leave you now, Miss Limrighton,' he said, bowing low, after he had seen all her wants attended to.

Constance gave him a dazzling smile, and Mr Evans went off to wait in the hall to waylay Lord Philip Cautry. Who would have thought old Ma Rider would have picked out such a lovely girl, thought Mr Evans disrespectfully. At least Lord Philip would be pleased. Now, there was a man with an eye for a well-turned ankle.

Left alone in front of the library fire, Constance ate an excellent supper, her appetite seeming still to be enormous. She looked doubtfully at the, as yet, untouched bottle of champagne. She had not taken any wine during her stay in London, remembering her aunt's strictures about it stinging like the adder and biting like the serpent. But she suddenly felt a small spark of rebellion. No one was here to see her. It would be discourteous not to drink any. She would just take one glass. How amusing that Mr Evans had called her Miss Limrighton! She wondered if he was in the habit of mistaking people's names. The champagne tasted refreshingly innocuous.

She looked around the library with a sudden pleasant feeling of well-being. A small pile of books with marbled covers lay on a table beside her. She idly picked one up and then let it drop. Novels! Constance had never read a novel — had never been allowed to read a novel. She drank another glass of champagne and warily picked it up. It was called *Cecilia*. She idly glanced at the first paragraph, looked closer, read — and then was lost in a dazzling world of fiction.

Down below, Mr Evans paced uneasily up and down the hallway. Lord Philip Cautry had not yet arrived and the *musicale* had begun, the high sexless voice of the male soprano echoing through the glittering rooms of the mansion.

He was just about to give up hope — Lady Eleanor had already done so — when the

51

door was opened and Lord Philip Cautry strolled in.

'Evening, Evans,' he remarked to the hovering secretary as the butler relieved him of his cloak and chapeau-bras. 'I have arrived at last, you see. Is my sister very angry?'

'Well, yes,' smiled Mr Evans. 'She had decided that you were not going to come.'

'Well, I am here at last and prepared to suffer the caterwauling. Lead the way.'

Mr Evans eyed him nervously. His lordship seemed in an unusually good humour. His normally harsh features were softened in a pleasant smile of unusual sweetness.

Mr Evans plucked up his courage. 'There *is* a little problem, my lord. There is this young lady, a Miss Limrighton, in the library and Lady Eleanor *commanded* me to arrange that you should meet this lady.'

'Oh, she did, did she?' drawled his lordship. 'Well, I ain't passing the evening with any Friday-faced, simpering miss of my sister's choice. Odd's life, Evans, you should know better than that.'

'Just so,' pleaded poor Mr Evans. 'But I have been *commanded*, my lord.' He looked up into Lord Philip's face like a whipped spaniel and his lordship sighed. Lord Philip could never bear to see anyone weak being bullied.

'Very well,' he sighed. 'I shall spend two seconds flat with her which means you will have fulfilled your part of the bargain.'

'Thank you,' said Mr Evans fervently. 'Oh, thank you, thank you very much, th . . .'

'Are you going to stand there all night thanking me?' demanded his lordship testily. 'Go on, man. Let's get it over with!'

Mr Evans hurriedly led the way to the library and threw open the door. 'Lord Philip Cautry,' he announced in a triumphant voice and, as Lord Philip walked passed him into the room, he gleefully closed the door behind him and ran off to tell Mr Rider the glad news.

Lord Philip raised his quizzing glass and surveyed the young lady seated beside the fire. She was so engrossed in the pages of a book that she had not even heard him being announced or was aware that anyone else was in the room.

He strolled lazily over to the fireplace and stood looking down at her. Constance suddenly became aware of another presence and her eyes flew upwards from the page and, with a frightened gasp, she let the book drop to the floor. She rose nervously to her feet and surveyed the man in front of her.

He was very tall with harsh, yet handsome

features. He wore his black hair long and confined at the back of his neck by a thin, black silk ribbon. His evening coat appeared to have been moulded to his broad muscular shoulders. His cravat was a miracle of sculptured perfection, and diamonds sparkled on his shoe-buckles and on his long white fingers. His eyes were heavy-lidded and as green as grass. There was no flicker of brown or hazel to mar his emerald stare, which was cat-like, unwinking and thoroughly unnerving.

Constance's eyes flew to the closed door and she gasped. 'Sir, we must observe the proprieties,' she said. 'The door is closed and I am unchaperoned.'

'That,' he said coldly, 'was, I gather, the idea, Miss Limrighton.'

'Why does everyone keep calling me Miss Limrighton?' said Constance. 'My name is Lamberton, Constance Lamberton.'

'Not Sir Edward's daughter?'

'Yes,' she said dutifully, 'Sir Edward was my father, and Lady Amelia Godolphin has given me the post of a companion to her, which is very kind and generous of her ladyship because without her charity I would starve,' she ended thankfully with the air of a child successfully reciting a lesson.

'You amaze me,' he said coldly. 'But it

seems there is some mistake. Poor Evans. He always does make a mull of things. You see, my sister wished him to arrange for me to meet a certain Miss Limrighton in private with a view to fixing my interest. It appears he fixed on the wrong lady. Allow me to introduce myself. I am Cautry, Lord Philip Cautry, at your service.'

Constance gave him a stricken look, 'Oh, I feel sure neither your sister nor Lady Amelia would wish me to be alone with you.' She threw another anguished look at the closed door.

'Do not fuss so,' he said testily. 'I am not in the habit of seducing virgins.'

'Why not?' asked Constance naively, the champagne suddenly rushing to her head and remembering all she had heard of the rakish Lord Philip. 'You seem to seduce everything else.'

'Bite your tongue, miss,' admonished his lordship with an amused glance towards the champagne bottle. 'Tell me instead how you came to have this post as companion.'

Constance was still wondering whether she had actually said the dreadful thing she thought she had just heard issuing from her own lips, but she marshalled her wits with a heroic effort and plunged into a long tale of the death of Aunt Maria and Lady Amelia's letter. Then she put a faltering hand up to her forehead as the full effect of the champagne hit her. 'I-I f-feel very faint,' she stammered. 'It's so hot in here.' She swayed and he caught her in his arms, looking down with amusement at the wide, magnificent hazel eyes which were staring dizzily up into his own, and despite himself he tightened his grip.

A faint seductive perfume came from the slight body in his arms and he realized with a slight shock that she smelled of soap. Extreme cleanliness in a female was a refreshing and exciting novelty, and it was only when she began to tremble slightly that he came to his senses and held her away from him.

'You are lucky, Miss Lamberton,' he said, 'that I am used to dealing with slightly tipsy debutantes. Sit down and calm yourself. We shall talk together until you feel more the thing.'

Constance sank down and buried her face in her hands. 'I am so ashamed,' she said in a muffled voice. 'Aunt told me not to touch wine. "At the last it biteth like a serpent and stingeth like an adder".'

'Just so,' commented his lordship with a blink. He was not used to females quoting the Bible, particularly after they had been held in his arms. 'But you will learn how to keep a clear head when you grow more accustomed to it. Now tell me, do you enjoy being a companion? You are well-treated?'

'Oh, yes,' lied Constance quickly. 'My duties are simply to chaperone Lady Amelia.'

'I am surprised that Amelia Godolphin should tolerate such a pretty companion.'

'Pretty! Me?' said Constance naively, 'Oh, *thank* you.'

Lord Philip sat down in the chair opposite and looked at her thoughtfully. Certainly the girl was elegantly gowned and coiffured. It appeared there was a softer side to the fair Amelia he had not discovered before.

'I knew your father well,' he said, leaning back in his chair. 'I can remember you — just. You were a pretty little thing. Always hiding behind chairs when I and my noisy friends would come to call. Sir Edward was a great huntsman but, I fear, an inveterate gambler. Was your aunt kind to you?' he asked abruptly.

'In her way,' said Constance slowly. Her head was beginning to clear and it felt strangely natural to be sitting talking to this elegant lord. 'She was very strict, and we read nothing but the Bible and Mr Porteous's sermons, you know.'

'Sounds curst dull,' commented Lord

Philip. 'Well that's all over now. A girl of your age should be enjoying balls and parties. Have you attended Almack's?'

'Oh, no,' said Constance. 'I fear Lady Amelia has not been granted vouchers.'

'That doesn't surprise me,' he said drily. 'Would you care to go?'

'Of course,' said Constance with a sudden infectious grin lighting up her face. 'Who wouldn't?'

'Perhaps I can arrange something,' he said slowly. 'I have some influence with the Patronesses.'

'Lady Amelia would be so delighted!' said Constance, clapping her hands and thinking to herself that a happy Amelia might be a more amiable mistress.

'Very well,' he said rising to his feet. 'I shall try. Now I must join the party or my sister will never forgive me. I shall escort you.'

'No, oh no! You mustn't,' cried Constance in alarm. 'Lady Eleanor told Lady Amelia I had not been invited and that there was no room available for me and asked — Mr Evans, is it? — to put me somewhere until the entertainment is over.'

Lord Philip's mouth folded in a hard line. 'I am sure you are mistaken,' he said grimly. He held out his hand. 'Come!'

But Constance held her ground. It was not the formidable Lady Eleanor who frightened her but Lady Amelia. She guessed shrewdly that Lady Amelia would be incensed to see her companion in the company of the man she hoped to marry.

'I am still feeling unwell, my lord,' she said firmly. 'I would be much happier staying here. Do *please* go.'

'Very well,' he said, looking at her thoughtfully. Constance stared up into those green eyes and felt a strange fluttering feeling in her stomach and a weakness in her legs but put it down to the effects of the champagne.

Lord Philip made her a courtly bow and left.

The *musicale* had finished and the guests had congregated in the supper room. He paused on the threshold. His sister came sailing up to meet him.

'So you have finally deigned to arrive, dear brother,' she said, kissing the air somewhere in the region of his cheek.

'I have been here for some time and I have been most charmingly entertained,' said Lord Philip with a mocking smile. 'I dropped into the library on my way and who should I meet but little Constance Lamberton . . .' his voice grew harder '. . .

banned from the festivities by some toplofty cow.'

'How dare she!' spluttered Lady Eleanor. 'She was not invited, and she is nothing more than a kind of servant.'

'*She* did not describe you so,' said her brother grimly. 'The description is mine alone, I assure you, and it fits you very well. You make so many people unhappy by your snobbery, Eleanor. It was a shabby thing to do!'

'How dare you preach manners to me,' gasped his sister, her face becoming mottled. 'George shall speak most strongly to you.'

'Don't go bullying poor George, and don't fuss Evans either with your plots and plans to marry me off. When I take a bride it will be someone of my own choosing and not some simpering, inbred milk-and-water miss.'

'No,' sneered Lady Eleanor. 'Some light-skirt like Amelia Godolphin, no doubt.'

'Amelia Godolphin has at least a kind heart where Miss Lamberton is concerned,' said Philip. He saw Amelia approaching and gave her his warmest smile. Amelia smiled back at him from under her long lashes and he caught his breath. She really was the most beautiful woman he had ever seen. He turned his well-tailored shoulder on his fulminating sister.

'Walk with me a little, Lady Amelia,' he said, taking her arm. He was about to relate his meeting with Constance but something prompted him to hold his tongue. Amelia thought her rages and jealous scenes well hidden, and would have been amazed to know that they were frequently talked about in about every polite drawing-room in London. Instead he said, 'I hear that you have engaged Miss Lamberton as companion.'

'Yes, indeed,' sighed Amelia. 'She is rather a tiresome little girl, but she is by way of being a relative and, my dear lord, she had no home — utterly destitute — I felt I had to do something for her. Of course, she could have just lived with me, but then, these terribly religious girls feel they must earn their bread. La! She is forever quoting scriptures. I fear she thinks I am shameless.'

'And are you?' teased Lord Philip in a light voice, but looking down into her beautiful face with such intensity that she felt a pleasurable thrill.

She gave a delicious trill of laughter and cast down her eyes.

'I am *eminently* respectable, my lord,' she

said, giving his arm a playful rap with her fan.

'I am very pleased with your concern for little Miss Lamberton,' he said in a low voice. 'I would be honoured if you would allow me to drive you tomorrow. Shall we say three o'clock?'

'Delighted,' murmured Amelia, keeping her eyes lowered to hide their triumphant gleam. So Mrs Besant had been right after all! The little Lamberton had her uses.

When Constance, much sobered, finally was allowed to leave the library and return home with Lady Amelia, she was surprised to note that her mistress was in a singularly charitable mood. Not only that. When the Comte Duval made one of his late-night calls, he was firmly told that my lady was too fatigued to receive him.

Perhaps, thought Constance, my life in London will not be so bad after all.

Chapter Five

In the following days, Lady Amelia's seemingly rapid rise to respectability amazed social London.

She was often seen in the company of that notoriously high-stickler, Lord Philip Cautry, and always chaperoned by Miss Constance Lamberton. Miss Lamberton's late papa had been a trifle rake-helly, chattered the dowagers, but no one could deny that Miss Lamberton herself was a very prim and proper miss.

Amelia's cup of happiness was full when, only a week after the *musicale,* vouchers arrived from the haughty Patronesses of Almack's for both herself and Constance. Amelia opened her purse-strings wide to buy herself the most expensive and elaborate toilette in London — to Constance's immeasurable relief, since it gave her a brief holiday from her constant dress-making.

With the exception of the butler, the servants at the house in Manchester Square had come to respect the quiet and well-bred Constance. And although Constance sometimes felt her life was not her own, being, as she was, at Amelia's autocratic beck and call from morning till night, her days began to seem easier than they had ever been since the death of her father. Added to that, she was cheered by the continued absence of the Comte Duval.

And if she occasionally wondered why she felt so breathless and shy in the presence of Lord Philip, she put it down to her own naivety. Lord Philip was, after all, one of the most fashionable leaders of the London scene, and almost rivalled Mr Brummell in social power.

Lady Amelia was particularly charming to Constance when Lord Philip was present, and Constance sincerely hoped that Lord Philip would marry Amelia, transferring her own half awakened, first trembling feelings of love for the handsome lord into duty.

For Constance did not know she had fallen in love with Lord Philip at that first meeting in the library. She only knew it was right and proper and *dutiful* to wish the best for her mistress. And Constance certainly believed Lord Philip to be the best.

Although no novice when it came to dealing with the fair sex, Lord Philip found himself becoming increasingly enamoured of Lady Amelia. She had persuaded him that her 'affair' with the Duke of Glendurran had merely been a misguided flirtation, and Society, in its usual wicked way, had believed the worst. He rarely noticed the quiet constant companion whose dark beauty was overshadowed by the more flamboyant colouring, dress and manners of her mistress.

It was he who had prevailed on the Patronesses to issue the prized vouchers.

He was preparing for the ball which was to be Lady Amelia's first Wednesday appearance at Almack's for some years, when his friend, the Honourable Peter Potter, was announced.

Peter Potter tried to aspire to the same heights of elegance as his friend, but he was notoriously absentminded, and Lord Philip, looking at his friend as he tied his cravat, was amused to notice that Peter was wearing an impeccable black evening coat and a snowy cravat atop a pair of canary coloured Inexpressibles and Hessian boots.

'You'll never get past the door of Almack's in that rig,' said Lord Philip, tying his cravat in an intricate combination of the Irish and the Mathematical — two collateral dents and two horizontal ones.

'What's up with it?' said Peter, wandering vaguely around his lordship's dressing-room and nearly tripping over a small table. 'I look all the crack. Weston made it.'

'Your trousers, man,' said Lord Philip patiently. 'Even the Prince Regent couldn't get into Almack's with trousers on, you know.'

Peter glanced down at his legs and then stared at his canary yellow trousers as if he could not believe his eyes. He was a tall, thin young man with a shock of fair hair and a weak, pleasant face like that of an amiable sheep. 'Gad's Oonds!' he said, still gazing in horror at his nether limbs. 'I don't know what servants are coming to these days. I told him to lay out my breeches. But he will no doubt be along presently.'

Peter's excellent valet was in the habit of following after his master with a valise full of clothes in order to remedy whatever fashionable disaster his absentminded master had thrown on before leaving the house.

'I hear you're about to be leg-shackled,' went on Peter, abruptly forgetting about the trousers and collapsing his long, bony length into a chair. 'It's not often I remember gossip, and I don't remember who told me except that it was several people and I said to myself, I said, "Not old Philip," I said, "Mistress, yes. Wife, no." Not that she isn't beautiful, but then so was that opera dancer you had in keeping. Anyway, that's what I said. Although she is trying so hard to become respectable — even dragging that poor little companion around with her at all hours, and all that bullying. *You* know, "Fetch me my shawl, Miss Lamberton. Oh, Constance, don't yawn. I declare you are the worst bore. I have dropped my fan, Miss Lamberton. Pick it up! You must remember your duties." Sickening, I think, don't you? So you can't possibly want to marry that. So *that's* all right. Are you going to Watier's tonight after the ball? You know, it don't look at all like you. I mean, standing there with your mouth open. I mean . . .'

'What on earth are you maundering on about?' snapped Lord Philip, who had, indeed, been staring at his garrulous friend in amazement. He had not heard the first part of the monologue, only the end. 'Has someone been saying I'm going to wed Constance Lamberton?'

'No. Though you could do a lot worse. Have you noticed her eyes? Well, I have. I am a great connoisseur of beauty,' he ended, simply and infuriatingly.

'Peter,' said his lordship, sitting down in a

chair opposite. 'I have been paying Lady Amelia a great deal of attention. Is that who you mean?'

'Of course,' said Peter vaguely, staring out of the window to where the parish lamps flickered and wavered in the blue dusk.

'I find Lady Amelia to be a charming and spirited girl of exceptional beauty who excites a great deal of spite and jealousy among less favoured ladies of the *ton*,' said Lord Philip severely. 'Perhaps the meek Miss Lamberton has put about these stories of bullying.'

'I wrote a poem about it,' said Peter, beginning to fish around in his pockets. 'Must be in my other coat.'

'About Lady Amelia?'

'Who? Oh, *her*. No. Twilight in London. Very moving. I remember it begins . . .'

But fortunately for Lord Philip, Peter's gentleman's gentleman appeared with the missing breeches. Peter wandered off into the bedroom to change, and Lord Philip wondered why a bit of the anticipation he had felt had fled. That was the trouble with these mealy-mouthed, religious little girls who were forever quoting scripture, thought Lord Philip nastily, forgetting that Constance had only quoted the Bible once, they always found someone to set up to play the bully. He felt quite disappointed in Constance.

Unaware of Lord Philip's angry feelings towards her, Constance sat demurely at Almack's that evening with the other chaperones and admired him from afar as he danced with Lady Amelia to a sprightly Scottish reel. He had an excellent leg, thought Constance dreamily, but it was a pity that he so often looked — well, *Satanic*, with his jet black hair, high-nosed white face and those odd, glittering green eyes.

Amelia's blonde beauty looked as delicate and fragile as porcelain as she weaved nimbly round Lord Philip in the figure eight.

They shall soon be married, thought Constance, and perhaps Lady Amelia will ask me to be her bridesmaid. I shall make myself . . . oh . . . ever such a pretty dress and perhaps Lord Philip will notice . . . 'Will notice what?' demanded a savage voice in her mind. 'He never notices you now, so why should he even notice you at his own wedding.'

And Constance flushed slightly and felt very sad, and did not yet know why.

Lord Philip happened at that moment to glance across the room at her. The flush on her cheeks lent her face some much needed colour and she looked young and remarkably beautiful as she sat studying the figures on her painted fan among the older, turbanned chaperones. Her dress was of a misty, smokey blue muslin which had formerly belonged to Amelia. Her creamy shoulders rose above the low neckline and her jet black hair was pinned in a demure little coronet on top of her small head. She wore no jewellery, but had pinned a little bunch of fresh violets in her hair. She had the fragile, translucent beauty of a spring flower.

Lord Philip gazed down at Lady Amelia who was pirouetting under his raised arm and frowned. He suddenly wished Amelia would not wear quite so much jewellery or such revealing dresses.

Before the dance separated them, he asked, 'Why is Miss Lamberton sitting with the dowagers? Does she not approve of dancing?'

All Amelia had to do was say, 'Yes,' and Lord Philip's slight interest in Constance Lamberton would have died. But Amelia considered Philip to be very high in the instep and wished to appear equally so. 'Her place is with the chaperones,' she said haughtily. 'She is merely fulfilling the duties for which she is paid.'

With that she tripped off in the figure of the dance and left Lord Philip to perform his part while his busy mind began to consider the implications of what she had said.

He did not wish to ask Constance to dance himself — he was very aware of his rank and his old name, and someone of his standing did not seek out little companions at Almack's. But Peter, now, never noticed who he was dancing with — or so Lord Philip believed. Anyway, he owed it to the memory of Constance's dead father to at least see that she was socially entertained.

He found Peter dreamily propping up a pillar under the musician's gallery. Peter was not a popular partner for he frequently forgot which lady he had asked to dance.

'Peter — you are not engaged at present. Why do you not ask Miss Lamberton for a dance?' said Lord Philip.

'Why not ask her yourself?' countered Peter lazily.

'Because I am already engaged to dance with several other ladies,' said Philip. 'Go to it, man. You said, after all, that she had beautiful eyes.'

'So I did,' said Peter. 'Where is she? Ah! She looks just like a London twilight in spring, all smokey blue and gold.'

Lord Philip stared insolently across the

room at Constance who lowered her eyes. 'I don't see any gold,' he remarked.

'Her eyes,' said Peter. 'Her eyes have little gold flecks in them. I shall go and have a closer look.'

He ambled off and Lord Philip gave his retreating back an indulgent smile. He hoped Peter would remember that the next dance was a quadrille and not try to perform the waltz!

But the quadrille was a new dance and Constance had not learned the steps which looked very baffling and intricate, more like a miniature ballet than a dance. She felt sure she could have acquitted herself tolerably well in a country dance, for she had learned the figures of most of them a long time ago when she was a little girl. So she hung her head and explained softly that she had not yet learned to dance the quadrille.

'Then I shall sit and talk to you,' said the amiable Peter, pulling forward a little gilt rout chair and placing it so that his back was to the ballroom and he was directly facing Constance.

'Your eyes are very beautiful,' he said.

'Thank you,' said Constance in an embarrassed voice and becoming aware of the stares of the dowagers next to her.

'Mr Pope says,' went on Peter, stretching

out his long legs, ' "True ease in writing comes from art, not chance, as those move easiest who have learned to dance." Do you agree? I ask because I am a poet, you see.'

Constance searched her mind feverishly for something witty and scintillating to say to this odd young man but finally came up with 'Oh!'

'Ah, so you say! So you say!' cried Peter, leaving Constance with the horrible thought that she had said something completely different. 'But you see I believe in inspiration. Sometimes I sit for days and not a word comes to me and then — Boom! — my fickle Muse bends to my ears and whispers divine words.'

'I cannot imagine a Muse saying "Boom!" ' said Constance.

'She doesn't *say* "Boom!" She *appears* like a . . . a . . . a muffin man ringing his curst bell.'

Constance began to giggle helplessly, wondering if they were both mad.

'Pray you, sir,' she gasped finally, 'say your Muse appears like a flash of lightning . . . or . . . or a golden bird alighting on your shoulder, but — oh, dear — the muffin man!'

'Very good, very good,' said Peter producing a small, grimy piece of paper from the pocket of his evening coat and a piece of

73

lead pencil. 'Let me see . . . what was that? Ah! Golden bird . . . yes, *very good.* You have a good ear, Miss . . . er . . . never mind, I shall read my latest poem to you. It is called "Twilight in London"'. He searched frantically about his person and then heaved a sigh. 'I have it not. No matter. I shall call on you as soon as possible.'

'May I know your name, sir,' ventured Constance, slightly embarrassed by this young eccentric but glad of his company.

'I am Peter Potter. I am a friend of Philip. You know, Cautry. Chap over there with green eyes like a parrot.'

'Cat,' said Constance gently. 'Cats have green eyes, Mr Potter. I think parrots have black eyes.'

'We shall make a marvellous team,' said Peter. 'Your imagery and my genius. Oh, it is the waltz. Famous! We shall dance.'

'I cannot,' said Constance dismally. 'I have not been given permission, and in any case I do not know the steps of the waltz any more than I know the steps of the quadrille.'

'Oh, the waltz is easy. You just follow me. But I shall find permission first.'

And to Constance's surprise that is exactly what Peter did. He did it by way of interrupting Lady Jersey in the middle of her favourite anecdote and saying, 'I wish to ask

74

Miss Lamberton to dance. You do not object? Good. Good!' and with that he ambled off leaving Lady Jersey, who had not said a word, to stare after him.

Constance timidly took the floor. She was sure Amelia would be annoyed with her for dancing, but, on the other hand, Mr Potter was Amelia's future husband's closest friend.

For all his eccentricity, Peter turned out to be a remarkably good dancer and an even better teacher, and soon Constance was floating round happily in his bony arms, oblivious of Lord Philip Cautry's sudden stare and Lady Amelia's raised eyebrows.

Constance was slightly disappointed when the dance ended, but Peter was still at her side. He took his former chair and seemed to have settled in for the evening.

'What a beautiful fan,' he said, taking Constance's fan from her hands.

'It is the only thing I have of my late mother,' said Constance.

'Peter, a word with you if Miss Lamberton can spare you.'

Constance looked up quickly into the emerald eyes of Lord Philip Cautry.

'Certainly,' Peter got lazily to his feet and absentmindedly walked off with Lord Philip, still carrying Constance's fan.

'I am grateful to you for giving Miss Lamberton a dance,' said Lord Philip, as soon as they were out of earshot. 'But you are making such a play for the girl that everyone expects you to put up the banns.'

Peter made no reply. He had suddenly realized he was very hungry indeed. He forgot he was with Philip, he forgot he was still carrying Constance's fan. He saw the food in an adjoining room and headed straight for it with single-minded intent.

Lord Philip shook his head and let him go. He was used to his friend's eccentricities, and in fact tolerated a great deal of eccentricity from many of his aristocratic acquaintances but would have dismissed a servant on the spot for one hundredth of their vagaries of behaviour.

Meanwhile, Lady Amelia had decided that the time was ripe for a little genteel seduction. She could not flirt too openly with Lord Philip in the ballroom — but if she got him to return with her to her home, there she could really set the stage. Constance, of course, would have to be present, but that had not deterred her in the past.

She had one more dance with Lord Philip, her second, a circumstance which started the gossiping tongues wagging. As she curtsied to him at the end of the dance, she gazed up at him with a discreet invitation in her eyes. 'I am fatigued by all these people, my lord,' she murmured. 'But I am always prepared to receive favoured guests in my home later in the evening . . .' She let her voice trail away and lowered her long lashes.

'Then I hope I am a favoured guest,' replied Lord Philip, taking his cue. He was conscious of a feeling of relief. It was already eleven o'clock. Respectable, *marriageable* young ladies did not ask gentlemen to their home at such a late hour. He could have what he desired without marrying in order to get it.

Looking slyly up at him from under her lashes, Amelia saw the glint in his eye and wondered if she had gone too far, too soon.

No matter. When she had him alone — well, alone apart from Constance who didn't count, she would lure him on just enough to tease him into marriage!

Philip watched her leave and then went in search of Peter who was engaged in munching a plate of rather stale-looking sandwiches. He was fanning himself absentmindedly with Constance's fan. Lord Philip looked down at him with a smile of amusement curling his lips. 'My dear Peter,' he drawled. 'Have you joined the Macaroni set?'

'No!' said Peter, wildly looking down at his evening dress, expecting to find he had left something off or had put something too much on. 'No, I'm all right, you know. Ain't got high heels on my shoes, ain't got the skirt of my coat boned, ain't wearing a corset, ain't . . .'

'The fan,' said Lord Philip gently interrupting this inventory. 'You are fanning yourself with a lady's fan.'

Peter looked at the pretty, painted fan with its slender ivory sticks in some amazement. Then his face cleared. 'It's Miss Lamberton's,' he said. 'I shall call on her and return it.'

'Let me do it for you,' said the friend. 'I think you have paid Miss Lamberton quite enough attention for one evening!'

'Now you understand your instructions,' snapped Lady Amelia to Constance. 'You are to sit in that corner and not interfere by look or deed. I am desirous of wedding my Lord Cautry, and should you do aught to put a spoke in my wheel you will find yourself in the streets begging for your bread. Do you understand?'

'Yes, Amelia,' said Constance, biting her lip to repress a sigh. Lady Amelia was her old, taciturn self since their return from the ball. She did not know that Amelia had noticed for the first time how pretty her companion had become, and did not like it one bit.

'Say, "Yes, my lady",' ordered Amelia, 'and take those stupid looking things out of your hair.' She wrenched the violets from their moorings and threw them on the fire.

Amelia narrowed her blue eyes as she stared at her companion. Something must be done to dim the girl's looks. She rang the bell and demanded to see her lady's maid.

When Eliot appeared, Amelia turned her cold blue eyes on her. 'Eliot,' she commanded the lady's maid, 'You will go to my rooms with Miss Lamberton and make sure she changes into a dress befitting a chaperone. I have an old brown velvet which should do quite well. Hurry! I hear a carriage arriving.'

Lady Amelia was alone when Philip was ushered into the room. Amelia was torn between playing propriety and ringing for the tea tray, or offering my lord some strong drink to fortify him. She decided strong drink would answer better and informed her butler to fetch the brandy decanter. The brandy was excellent, better than Lord Philip had tasted for a long time.

'A present from one of my admirers,'

smiled Amelia in answer to his query.

'The Comte Duval, no doubt,' murmured Lord Philip. 'French brandy of this quality is hard to come by these days.'

'Well, he is my admirer no longer,' laughed Amelia. 'He is paying ardent court to that Friday-faced General's daughter, Fanny Braintree.'

Philip raised his eyebrows. 'Indeed! Then it is a good thing our dear comte is a royalist. Were he a Bonapartist one would suspect his intentions. The General corresponds frequently with Wellesley, you know.'

'Oh that silly war,' yawned Amelia, dismissing the whole Peninsular campaign. 'I wonder you want to talk about it, considering you spent two years in Spain and were wounded for your pains. Where were you wounded by the way? Anywhere that matters?'

Philip nearly dropped his glass. That was the sort of remark he would have expected from a Haymarket Cyprian. But he rallied quickly and was about to reply, when the door opened and Constance came quietly into the room. Philip got to his feet and bent punctiliously over her hand, and then returned her fan to her.

'Oh, thank you!' cried Constance with a radiant smile ('Just as if she were getting the crown jewels,' thought Amelia bitterly, 'and just wait until I get my hands on Eliot!')

For the lady's maid's idea of suitable attire for a companion was, indeed, a brown velvet dress, but not the old one that Amelia had meant. This was more gold than brown, high-waisted in the current mode and with a little stiff collar of gold lace at the neck. It brought out the gold flecks in Constance's large eyes and flattered her slight figure.

Constance caught Amelia's angry stare and retired to a ladder-backed chair in the far corner of the room with her work basket, took out her sewing, and proceeded to work diligently.

Amelia was sitting on a gilt and painted sofa which she had bought after seeing David's painting of Madame de Recamier reclining on one like it. She leaned against the bolster cushion at one end and patted the space beside her invitingly. 'Come and sit by me . . . Philip,' she said, looking at him with a lazy seductive smile.

Lord Philip glanced over at Constance but that young lady's head was bent over her sewing and she did not look up. 'She has been through this before,' he thought suddenly.

But this pretty bird of paradise waiting for him so eagerly on the sofa was not to be ignored. He resolutely put Constance from his mind and sat down next to Amelia.

She promptly leaned against him and put her hand on his knee. He slid his arm round her waist and drew her close. It was then that he looked over her gold head and met Constance's wide and troubled gaze.

He suddenly felt as if someone had poured a bucket of cold water over him. How could he proceed with this affair while the innocent daughter of one of his old friends looked on?

So he bent and kissed Amelia briefly on the cheek. 'And now I must go,' he said abruptly, releasing her and rising to his feet.

'Your most humble servant, Lady Amelia.' He made a magnificent leg and then turned briefly towards Constance and bowed. 'I bid you good evening, Miss Lamberton. Mr Potter will be happy to know that I have delivered your fan.'

And then with a small, general bow to both ladies, he turned and walked from the room. Amelia ran after him into the hall and grasped his arm.

'Come now, Philip,' she cried in a breathless voice. 'I fear I have shocked you. I am perhaps too much accustomed to the freer ways of a married woman. But, nonetheless, I shall make some gentleman a very good wife, think you.'

'Undoubtedly,' said Lord Philip, gently detaching himself, 'I assure you, I enjoyed my visit and I am pleased to see Miss Lamberton in such good looks. Goodnight, Lady Amelia . . . again.'

The street door banged. He was gone.

'Constance!' called Lady Amelia. 'Come here!'

Constance appeared in the doorway of the drawing-room, her wide eyes looking questioningly at Lady Amelia. Amelia's jealous eyes raked her from head to toe.

'Turned very fine, haven't you?' she sneered. 'But you are to stop wearing my clothes, miss, and in future wear your own. Fine feathers make fine vultures. So Lord Philip Cautry thinks you are in good looks. Well, we'll see what our high and mighty Lord thinks of you next time he sees you! Oh, go to bed. That stupid face of yours makes me feel *sick!*'

She stared furiously at Constance as the girl moved past her to mount the stair, unconscious grace in every line and movement. Amelia had consumed too much brandy, and her never stable temper broke completely. As Constance was beginning to mount the stairs, Amelia seized a carriage whip from the hall stand and lashed

Constance across the back with it so viciously that the wicked thong slashed through the fine velvet of the dress and cut into the girl's flesh.

Constance swung round, her face parchment-white and her eyes glittering with rage. She slowly walked towards her mistress.

'Bergen!' called Amelia, summoning the butler before Constance could reach her. The butler scuttled forward as if he had been waiting in the shadows. 'Make sure Miss Lamberton finds her room,' said Amelia, breathing hard. 'The house is still strange to her and I fear she may become lost.'

'Very good, my lady,' said Bergen with a slow smile. Constance stared at the ill-assorted pair, the butler with his sinister smile and Lady Amelia with her beautiful face contorted with rage and malice and spite.

The full shock of the attack on her struck her, and Constance turned and fled. She ran as hard as she could to her rooms and only when she had barricaded the door, did she allow herself the luxury of bursting into tears, sitting on the bed with her arms wrapped tightly round her middle, rocking herself back and forth in an agony of pain

and humiliation, crying over and over again
to the uncaring silk-covered walls, 'What is
to become of me? How can I escape? What
can I do?'

Chapter Six

Lord Philip Cautry was angry with Miss Constance Lamberton. Looking back on his evening at Amelia's in the damp, sober light of a misty London afternoon, he finally came to the conclusion it was all Constance's fault. What right had she to play Miss Propriety? No one could live for longer than a day with Amelia and not realize she had the morals of a cat, thought his lordship sourly, forgetting that he had only too recently considered Amelia innocent of the scandal that surrounded her name.

He had been celibate for over a year and had been happily on the point of putting an end to that uncomfortable state. He felt somewhere in the back of his mind that Amelia hoped for marriage. But didn't they all? Even the little opera dancer that he had kept in such style for several months some time ago had begun to show alarming signs that she wished to legalize the romance. The effrontery of some women was past all believing, thought Lord Philip. He came from an ancient family and had no intention of tainting his family tree with doubtful branches of the Fashionable Impure.

Miss Constance Lamberton would just have to learn the ways of the world and not sit around like some sort of chaste angel giving gentlemen of the *ton*, hell-bent on seduction, a guilty conscience.

He voiced as much to his friend, Peter, when that young man called round to see him. Peter was wearing an impeccably tailored blue swallowtail coat of Bath superfine. His waistcoat was a subdued rose colour, his pantaloons were without a crease and his cravat was a miracle of starched perfection. But he had spoiled the whole effect by forgetting to put on his boots, and his long narrow feet were encased in a pair of red Morocco slippers.

'Don't think that's the case,' said Peter after much hard thought. 'Amelia is said to keep Constance with her the whole time — even when she's playing hot-in-the-hand in her drawing-room with the Comte Duval.'

'I think the prim Miss Lamberton may be a malicious gossip,' said Lord Philip. 'Must you pick your teeth with the end of your quizzing glass, Peter? Sometimes your mannerisms are just as irritating as Miss Lamberton's stately virginity. And you have forgot your boots, man. You're wearing your slippers.'

'No. Not Miss Lamberton. Amelia's lady's maid is related to my cook, and *she* told my second footman who told my butler who told my valet. So there! I'm not picking my teeth. I'm polishing 'em. And damn my slippers. What's that man of mine about? But I suppose he'll be along directly,' said Peter, replying to each of Lord Philip's points in turn.

Lord Philip's thin eyebrows raised in distaste. 'Servants' gossip, Peter. I had thought better of you. A gentleman should never listen to servants' gossip.'

'Why not?' exclaimed Peter in surprise, removing the end of the quizzing glass from his mouth and beginning to scratch his head with it. 'I always do. I wouldn't dream of having my morning chocolate without it,' he added with the air of someone advocating rhubarb pills. 'I like your coat. Weston, I suppose. I wish they would take away that little bag at the back of the neck. No need for it now. It ain't as if we still wear periwigs. Come to think of it, your own hair's too long for a man of fashion. Why don't you get a

Brutus crop? Then you wouldn't have to tie it back in that bow. Mine is called the Windswept. Do you like it?'

'What's left of it,' said his lordship dryly, watching the quizzing glass wrecking havoc with the hairdresser's art. 'Why don't you use that thing properly? You're supposed to look through it. But, by George, you've done every other curst thing. Why don't you scratch your armpits?'

'You're in love with her. That's what's making you so twitty,' said Peter, rising to meet the arrival of his man with his boots.

'Don't be ridiculous!' snapped Lord Philip. 'I may have a certain *tendre* for Amelia Godolphin. But I am certainly not in love with her.'

'I meant Constance,' said Peter. But by that time he had drifted off into the other room to have his boots pulled on and so his words went unheard by Philip.

Lord Philip was cursed with the tenacity of the typical English aristocrat — a single-minded pursuit of the desired goal. He wanted to bed Lady Amelia; he was vaguely surprised that Constance should annoy him so much. But nonetheless, he wanted Lady Amelia and meant to have her.

He accordingly crossed to the fireplace and took down several cards from the card stand and began to flick through them. His sister was holding a breakfast which had already begun, since the hour was now four in the afternoon and all fashionable breakfasts began at three. He cordially detested his sister, but he felt sure that Amelia would somehow manage to be there. He collected his hat and his cane and set out, forgetting his friend, Peter, with an absent-mindedness worthy of that gentleman himself.

The breakfast was to be held at his sister's villa in Kensington where she could erect marquees on the lawn for eating and dancing which she could not do in the pocket-sized garden which graced the back of her town house.

Kensington, with its pretty villas lining the Chiswick Road, was soon reached. It had all the charm of being not quite in town and not quite in the country. The mist had dispersed to be replaced with a grey drizzle. Water dropped from the great trees by the side of the road, and sooty sparrows squabbled and splashed in the puddles.

As soon as he arrived, Philip could sense that the occasion was not a success. Although the marquees were bedecked with flowers and draped with rose silk, the damp grey day seemed to have permeated everything. The reason was quickly discovered.

His sister had turned her autocratic face from strong drink and had decided to serve only negus, ratafia and lemonade.

He found his sister, twisting the fringe of her shawl nervously in her fingers and fighting between her strong principles and the desire to make her breakfast a success. Philip looked at her worried face with some amusement as she surveyed her nearly silent guests.

'Give in,' he said gently, 'or it will be all over London on the morrow that you have turned Methodist.'

'Oh, no,' cried Lady Eleanor, 'they wouldn't *dare!*'

'The trouble with this curst affair,' came the booming voice of one of the guests, the elderly Earl of Murr, 'is it's damn wet and dreary outside and curst damp, wet and dreary on the inside of m'stomach.'

'Evans!' bleated Lady Eleanor desperately. 'Go and *command* the butler to bring out the *best* claret, champagne, and port. I don't know what he can be thinking of.'

She waited anxiously until the footmen started circulating with the stronger drink. Soon a happy buzz of conversation filled the marquee and she sighed with relief.

'It was all Evans's fault, of course,' said Lady Eleanor with restored complacency, 'and so I shall tell everyone.'

'Nonsense!' said Philip, helping himself to wine. 'Do that and I shall counter it with the truth. I don't think you really appreciate Evans. I am looking for a secretary myself, you know.'

Lady Eleanor blanched. She was able to bully her meek husband on most matters. But Mr Rider was devoted to his secretary, and she shuddered to think of his reaction should his main prop be taken from him. He might even refuse to fund her social engagements! 'You shall not take Evans from me. Besides he wouldn't go. Only last night Mr Rider said he was going to pay him more money. Didn't you, dear?' She nudged her husband in the ribs and he roused himself and said, 'Yes, yes,' although he hadn't heard a word.

And so a much gratified Evans was informed that further to their discussion of the night before, his salary would be raised immediately and with the cunning of the timid, Mr Evans did not show any surprise that Lady Eleanor should be talking so long and so vehemently about a nonexistent discussion of his salary.

He had, in fact, nearly lost his job earlier that day despite the championship of Mr Rider when Lady Eleanor had discovered that once again Lady Amelia's name was featured on her guest list, and it took all Evans's tact and nimble ability to lie to explain to her that the Countess Lieven had expressed *a particular wish* to see Lady Amelia at the function. For all her overbearing ways, Lady Eleanor was naive and it never crossed her mind for a moment that the quiet and trustworthy Mr Evans could be lying, and that an arrogant social leader like the Countess Lieven who declared 'It is not fashionable where I am not,' would ever consider showing an interest in Lady Amelia. Mr Evans had, in fact, simply used the same guest list as the one for the *musicale*.

The guests were becoming increasingly noisy since they had been drinking wine steadily, in the way a hard-drinking society will if it has been deprived of its favourite beverage for over an hour.

Lord Philip raised his quizzing glass and stared across the tent at Amelia who demurely lowered her eyes. She was wearing a morning dress of scarlet taffeta cut low enough to show the world that she was possessed of an excellent pair of shoulders. Then to his irritation, he found his eyes drawn to the quiet companion by Lady Amelia's side. What a quiz of a dress! It was a brown silk and he could swear it was actually patched neatly on one of the sleeves. Constance's face was white, almost translucent, like alabaster, and her large eyes briefly held such an expression of pain and bewilderment that Lord Philip dropped his own eyes and fortified himself from the bottle at his elbow, feeling strangely uneasy.

He was unaware that Mrs Besant had been watching him like a hawk.

'Things are beginning to happen,' thought that malicious widow gleefully. She turned her avid gaze on Constance who was now toying with her food.

That dress was one of the girl's old ones, thought Mrs Besant happily. But was she cold? She kept pulling her shawl up round her bare shoulders in an oddly protective way.

The sound of fiddles came from the other marquee across the lawn as Neil Gow and his famous musicians, hired specially for the day, began to tune up. One by one the guests began to rise to their feet. Lady Amelia got up and said something to Constance in a sharp voice. The girl dutifully rose and left the tent one pace behind her mistress, but not before Mrs Besant's eagle eyes had caught the veiled look of anger mixed with fear that Constance had cast on Amelia, or the way the girl moved her shoulders stiffly as if she were in pain.

Mrs Besant hurried after them. A pale, watery sunlight was filtering through a grey veil of cloud and the day had turned warm and humid. Roses bloomed in every corner of the garden, glittering with rain, their heavy heads hanging down under the weight of the rainwater. As Mrs Besant hurried up behind her, a thorn caught in Constance's shawl and pulled it down, away from her back and neck.

And Mrs Besant drew in her breath with a sharp hiss of satisfaction. A long, savage red weal was cut across the girl's white shoulders. Constance quickly untangled her shawl and huddled it around her shoulders.

Mrs Besant stopped her pursuit and turned instead to go in search of Lord Philip.

Lord Philip was often considered too proud and toplofty by many of society but Mrs Besant, watching the charming smile that lit up his lordship's rather austere features as he bent his black head to listen to something that grubby little secretary was saying, thought that, on the contrary, there were times when Lord Philip Cautry was *too* democratic.

Ignoring the secretary completely, she

rudely broke into their conversation with, 'Cautry! A word in your ear.'

'I am talking to Mr Evans, Mrs Besant,' said Lord Philip in arctic tones, 'or perhaps you hadn't noticed.'

Mrs Besant gave the secretary a smile. Mr Evans reflected that although he had been told the human mouth usually holds thirty-two teeth, God had seen fit to give Mrs Besant fifty. They seemed to snap at him awfully as if they had a separate life of their own, and with an incoherent mumble he took his leave.

'What is it?' said Lord Philip, staring down at Mrs Besant with distaste. She was only a vicar's daughter after all, and it was time someone put her in her place.

But her opening words caught his full attention.

'I am really surprised to see a fine and brave gentleman like yourself stand by while Miss Constance Lamberton — who is, after all, the daughter of an old friend of yours — is whipped.'

'Come now,' snapped Philip, angry at the sudden feeling of foreboding that had assailed him. 'You have been reading too many gothic novels, Mrs Besant.' But he did not walk away.

'Then ask her,' breathed Mrs Besant,

moving close to him and speaking in a murmur, 'ask her where she got that cruel whiplash on her back!' She smiled, giving him the full benefit of her array of yellow teeth, gave a jerky little nod of her head, and then began to speak in a high voice about something completely different as she saw a little knot of guests approaching.

Lord Philip walked quickly in the direction that Amelia and Constance had taken. He was tired of all this gossip, these rumours. He suddenly remembered holding Constance in his arms, and looking down on the intriguing vista of white and flawless back revealed by her low evening gown.

The dance had not yet begun and Amelia and Constance were seated at a small table where more refreshments were being served. Amelia gave him a dazzling smile and waved him over to join them. A stray sunbeam shining through a small tear in the canvas lit up the pure, pale, white gold of her hair and Philip caught his breath. No one so beautiful could be so guilty of such cruelties.

Amelia launched into the latest *on-dit* and Lord Philip listened appreciatively since the story concerned a couple he did not like in the least. When Amelia had finished, Lord Philip turned his attention to Constance.

'Are you cold, Miss Lamberton?' he asked,

looking at Constance who sat with a Norfolk shawl huddled around her shoulders. Amelia had forgotten the whiplash, and only wanted Lord Philip to see what a drab Constance looked in that frumpy gown.

Before Constance could reply, Amelia said, 'Yes, Constance dear. It is so hot in here, but the way you are huddled up one would think we were at the North Pole.' And before Constance could stop her, Amelia had leaned forward and twitched the shawl from her shoulders and it fell to the ground. Constance bent quickly to retrieve it, and Lord Philip saw the ugly weal that marred the white skin of her back.

'Miss Lamberton,' he said in a flat, emotionless voice. 'That is a very ugly scar on your back. One would think someone had been taking a whip to you.'

Amelia gave a shrill laugh, 'It is a birth mark, isn't it, Constance dear?'

Constance looked straight at Amelia, her large, hazel eyes totally expressionless.

'No,' she said, baldly.

'Then how came you by it?' persisted Lord Philip.

Amelia became aware of her friend Mrs Besant, standing behind the chair listening avidly, and her pale blue eyes flashed a warning at Constance.

Constance rose gracefully to her feet. 'I am feeling a trifle unwell,' she said in a thin voice. 'If you will excuse me, Lady Amelia, I must go into the house.'

'By all means, Coz,' trilled Amelia, all mock solicitation. 'Lord Philip will chaperone me until your return.'

'Perhaps it would be better if I escorted Miss Lamberton home,' said Lord Philip, his green eyes fastened on Constance's pale face.

'Come, now!' laughed Amelia, laying a possessive hand on his arm. 'Such a fuss over a young girl's megrims. You gentlemen of the world must be aware that us ladies are plagued with the vapours at a *certain time of the month.*'

Constance blushed scarlet and fled. Lord Philip wondered for one awful moment if he, too, were blushing. Amelia couldn't possibly have meant . . . wouldn't have dared . . . no woman *ever* . . .

He was grateful for the presence of Mrs Besant, who plumped herself down in Constance's chair and leaned her knobby elbows on the table.

But Lord Philip's embarrassment was not over, for Mrs Besant was hell-bent on mischief.

'Tell me, dearest,' said Mrs Besant, leaning towards Amelia and flashing a look at Philip to make sure he was listening, 'Do, but do, *do* tell how little Constance got that simply terrible mark on her back. It looks just as if it had been made by someone striking her with a whip . . .'

Constance walked quickly into the Riders' large sprawling villa and began to breathe more easily as the noise of the party receded behind her. She simply wanted to be alone to sort out her anguished and very muddled thoughts. The cool quiet rooms seemed deserted, since both servants and masters were with the guests in the garden.

She pushed open a door at random and found herself in a large music room. Pale sunlight filtering through the trees outside the long windows dappled the polished oak floor. There was very little furniture apart from a large gilt harp, a prettily painted spinet, a few comb-and-splat Windsor chairs, and a Pembroke table holding a lustre bowl full of red and white roses.

Constance sat down on one of the chairs, bent her head and tried to marshal her thoughts. Despite Amelia's vicious attack on her, Constance felt disloyal to her mistress for harbouring such angry thoughts about her. For although Constance came from an ancient and respected English family, Amelia topped her in rank, and Constance had always been taught to respect her betters — betters, of course, meaning anyone higher up on the social scale. Then there was that stern matter of duty. She was employed by Amelia, therefore it was her duty to obey Amelia.

And under all these noble thoughts ran the fear of being turned out into the London streets. Constance had lived a grim but isolated life with her aunt, and had therefore been spared many of the horrible sights of the day.

In the less favoured areas of London, however, she expected to see the grim and scab-faced rabble with their wild eyes and filthy clothes. But it was the behaviour of her peers that shocked her. The cruelty of the young bucks and bloods who roamed the streets and squares of the West End, harassing the old and crippled and weak. She had once walked from the house escorted by Eliot, the lady's maid, to do some shopping in Bond Street and had been appalled at the behaviour of an extremely smart and elegant group of young men. As soon as Constance and the maid had come abreast of them, they had proceeded to make water against the railings of the square, sniggering and loudly calling her attention to their behaviour.

The darker pits of sexual behaviour which Amelia had tried to din into her unwilling ears had left her surprisingly untouched. There is, after all, no greater protection than a truly virginal mind.

She found her thoughts returning — as they did with increasing frequency these days — to Lord Philip. More and more had she begun to think him a fitting mate for her mistress, but more because Lord Philip seemed almost as wrapped up in the rank and honour of his name as Amelia was in her beauty. And yet . . . he had seemed so kind that splendid night he had held her in his arms. Just what a brother might do, thought Constance, severely pushing down more pleasurable feelings.

Was it so bad to be whipped by one's mistress? her busy brain rattled on. Servants were whipped, of course, and younger brothers and sisters. She was sure it was odd for a lady to take the whip to her companion, but then, she knew so little of the world. There was only one salvation for a girl like herself, she concluded sadly, and that was marriage. I would marry the first man who asked me, she thought. A home of my own and children of my own would make up for an absence of love.

Constance was so immersed in her thoughts that she had not heard the sound of someone entering the hall outside and approaching the door of the music room. She jerked her head up only as a strangely familiar voice said urgently, 'In here!'

Constance saw the doorknob beginning to turn and ran for the open windows. She stood on a small terrace outside, looking for a way down. But the terrace ran round the corner of the house and presumably there would be steps there. She was reluctant to walk past the window and expose herself in case the person in the room behind turned out to be the acid Mrs Besant, the haughty Lady Eleanor or even Amelia herself. She decided to stay quietly on the terrace, between the windows, until whoever it was should leave.

The conversation in the room behind her was in French and, although Constance recognized one of the speakers as the Comte Duval, she could not make out a word. Unlike many of her contemporaries, she did not know one word of French. She therefore had a comfortable feeling that she was not eavesdropping but amused herself by trying to recognize some of the words that sounded familiar. She heard the name, 'Fanny

Braintree' and then 'Bonaparte', then 'l'Empereur' — 'that must be Emperor,' thought Constance — then the word 'espion' repeated several times and then the word 'trahison'. The murmur of voices went on and Constance began to become anxious. Surely Lady Amelia would be looking for her by this time!

She decided she could not wait any longer. She ran nimbly to the end of the terrace, her little leather slippers making no sound, fled round the corner of the terrace and saw, with relief, a double flight of steps leading down into the garden.

But before she could reach them, the thorns of a rose bush growing in an urn on the terrace caught at the weak, worn leather strap of her fan and tore it from her wrist. She hesitated, wondering whether to wait and extricate her fan from the bush, but she heard the rapid, pursuing sound of footsteps coming from the direction of the music room, and fled into the garden.

The Comte Duval rounded the terrace and stood staring, his face quite pale under the paint. No one. He thought he saw the flicker of a skirt disappearing through the bushes but he could not be sure.

'Someone heard us?' said his companion, coming up behind him, speaking in English.

'She left this,' said the comte, slowly plucking Constance's fan from the rose bush. 'What shall we do, my little English friend?'

'We must flee!' babbled his companion. 'The game is up!'

'Quietly, *mon amie,* quietly. *Doucement!*' said the comte, swinging the fan back and forth in his long fingers.

'If she knows what we were saying, what we were plotting, she will raise a rumpus immediately and we can still escape. If there is no brouhaha in the next few minutes, she has not heard or understood, but nonetheless we dare not let her live. We must start to find out then who the owner of this fan is and when we find her, why, we kill her.'

'Oh, *no!*' bleated his companion.

'Oh, yes, my little English coward. You are now in too deep to draw back. We find her, we kill her. Life is very simple if you but take the proper action . . .'

Amelia had been too engrossed in her battle of wits with Mrs Besant to notice Constance's long absence. She had also practically forgotten the existence of Lord Philip Cautry who was heartily wishing himself elsewhere.

'And that *gown!*' Mrs Besant was saying.

'Surely you can do better for Miss Lamberton than *that*. I declare it has a patch on the sleeve.'

'She *likes* going around like a drab,' snapped Amelia. The sunlight winked on the diamond pendant at her neck, driving Mrs Besant to further attack.

'After all, dear Amelia,' murmured Mrs Besant. 'We all know 'twas exceeding kind of you to give the girl a home. But a roof over her head seems to be all she has. And you still have not told me how she came by that scar.'

'It's a birthmark!' said Amelia.

'A *birthmark!*' exclaimed Mrs Besant, showing all her teeth. 'Come, come! There wasn't a mark on her back at Almack's. Therefore she got it sometime *after* Almack's. When she went home, perhaps?'

Amelia took a deep breath and leaned across the table, pushing her pretty face almost into that of Mrs Besant and affording Lord Philip an excellent view of two large breasts revealed by her plunging neckline. 'I am surprised you had the time to notice,' she said silkily. 'The morning post takes up so much of your time.'

Mrs Besant reeled back in her chair and raised her hand like a fencer receiving a hit. 'Well, well,' she said breathlessly. 'I am sure

Lord Philip is bored with our women's chatter.'

'You must excuse me,' said Philip, taking the opportunity to escape. Amelia bit her lip. In her way, she enjoyed her verbal battles with Mrs Besant more than the attention of any man, but Lord Philip had the two things she desired most, money and a title. 'You are quite right,' she said, rising and slipping her arm through Philip's, 'and I shall promenade with you.'

Philip looked down at her enchanting face, and wondered why he had ever found her attractive. She was vulgar beyond belief and, if Mrs Besant's hints could be believed, she was also making life hell for that poor little Lamberton girl. His green eyes raked over the grounds for a way to get rid of her, and with relief, he espied the elegant, if foppish, figure of the Comte Duval.

'Monsieur le Comte,' he cried, before Amelia realized what he was about. 'I must beg you to escort Lady Amelia for me. I have business to attend to.'

'Indeed, I am delighted to relieve you of your beautiful charge,' said the comte, bowing low while Lord Philip wrinkled his nose fastidiously at the strong smell of musk emanating from that gentleman's clothes.

Philip bowed and left them. He found he

was becoming increasingly worried about Constance's welfare. He suddenly saw her walking under the trees with Peter Potter. She was laughing at something Peter had just said, her face alight with humour and mischief. 'Why, she is really pretty,' he thought in surprise. 'Almost beautiful. Now, were she married to someone suitable, it would solve all the problems. Peter, perhaps?'

At that moment, Peter caught Constance's hand and bent his long sheep-like face to kiss it, and Constance gently drew her hand away, her face turning pink with embarrassment.

No, Peter is too clumsy, he thought angrily. She needs someone stronger — more masculine — like . . . like . . .

'Like yourself?' whispered a mocking voice in his brain. 'Like *yourself?*'

Chapter Seven

The following day, Constance was informed by Eliot that she once more had the use of my lady's old clothes. And not only that, there was a letter for her!

Constance broke the unfamiliar seal and crackled open the parchment. She scanned it briefly and then began to read it more closely. It was from her late aunt, Miss Lamberton's heir, a Mr Nicholas Barrington.

'*Dear Miss Lamberton,*' she read. '*I am selling Berry House since the house itself is of no interest to me and the little land there is, is nothing more than a few impoverished fields. I heard from the vicar that Lady Amelia Godolphin had kindly offered you a home and I am glad your future is secure. Nonetheless, I and my wife shall be calling on you on the tenth of this month, since we wish to assure ourselves that you are comfortably situated. I remain yr.*

Humble and Obedient Servant, Nicholas Barrington.'

Constance's heart leapt with sudden hope. *Today* was the tenth! And Mr and Mrs Barrington were concerned over her welfare. She would *beg* them to take her with them. Perhaps they could employ her as a housekeeper, or if they had children, as a governess. But Amelia must not even guess at her hopes. She would simply tell her that they were to call and that she wished to remain at home to receive them.

Amelia greeted the news rather sulkily. There was a *fête champêtre* in the Surrey fields she wished to attend. She was looking forward to recommencing the pursuit of Lord Philip in that sylvan setting, and with even more pleasure she was looking forward to another verbal battle with Mrs Besant.

But if she did not let Constance stay to see these tiresome relatives, Mrs Besant was sure to find out about it somehow and use it as a weapon.

'Very well, then,' she said ungraciously. 'I see you are still wearing those terrible old clothes. Tell Eliot to find you something directly. I declare you go around looking like a quiz just to embarrass me!'

Constance restrained from pointing out that she was wearing her own clothes on

Amelia's express orders, and merely murmured her thanks.

Then came the agony of waiting. Amelia finally left in a flurry of silks and bad temper. Constance, attired in a pale yellow muslin gown tied under the breast with long yellow silk ribbons, sat demurely in the drawing-room, perched on the edge of her chair, starting at every sound of carriage wheels on the street outside.

Bergen, the butler, kept scuttling into the room on various pretexts, seeming to enjoy Constance's dislike and fear of him. At one point, as the butler's pale gooseberry eyes roved over her figure with blatant insolence, Constance felt she would have to give up her vigil and escape from the house, but all at once carriage wheels did stop outside, and Bergen scuttled off to answer the summons of the knocker.

But it was not Mr Barrington but Lord Philip Cautry who was ushered into the room.

Constance rose and curtsied low, determined to get rid of him as soon as possible. But his infuriating lordship seemed to be in no hurry. He sat down in a chair opposite and stretched out his long legs in front of him. He discussed the weather, the press of traffic in the streets outside, the latest *on-dits* while Constance stared at him in amazement. He seemed a positive chatterbox this morning.

'You are wondering why I have come,' he suddenly said abruptly.

'I-I assume you expected to find Lady Amelia at home,' rejoined Constance nervously.

'No. I came to see you, Miss Lamberton.' He rose and came to stand over her, his green eyes glinting like a cat's in the dim light of the room.

'How-h-ow nice,' said Constance faintly, her hand nervously feeling at her wrist for the strap of her fan and finding it missing.

'I am concerned about your position in this household,' he said, and immediately wondered if he sounded as pompous to her as he did to himself. 'I bear an old and honourable name, Miss Lamberton. I am offering you the protection of that name.'

The beautiful hazel eyes flew upwards in surprise and dismay. 'My lord,' said Constance. 'It is exceeding kind of you to offer me the protection of your name, but I assure you I am not yet reduced to such straits.'

Lord Philip stared down at her in amazement and fury. And then he realized she had misunderstood the great honour he was about to confer on her.

He knelt on one knee beside her chair and took her hand in his. 'Miss Lamberton,' he said, 'I am not asking you to be my mistress — but my wife.'

Constance looked at him in dazed bewilderment and then a slow, enchanting smile lit up her face. This was like all her girlhood dreams come true — this handsome lord kneeling beside her and proposing marriage. And if Lord Philip Cautry could have kept his aristocratic mouth shut, then Miss Lamberton would undoubtedly have accepted him on the spot.

But he felt compelled to add, 'I realize this will not be a love match, Miss Lamberton. I feel I owe it to your dear father's memory to see that his daughter is no longer ill-treated. My family will be surprised, of course. They will naturally have expected me to look higher for a bride. But, no matter. I will deal with them.'

A cloud settled down over the sunshine of Constance's face. There was a long and heavy silence. A hawker shouted his wares outside, the clock on the mantel ticked breathlessly on, and the shuffle of the butler's feet sounded in the hall outside.

At last Constance said, 'You do me great honour, my lord. But I fear I cannot accept.

You see, the relative who inherited my aunt's estate is calling today and I am determined to beg him to remove me from this household. I do not wish to be ungrateful to Lady Amelia, but, indeed, I am not happy here. I fear . . .'

She broke off as Lord Philip Cautry rose to his feet, his face as black as thunder. He had only heard her refuse him. She had refused none other than Lord Philip Cautry, he who had been fêted and petted and chased after by every matchmaking mama in London since he was first out of short coats.

'Then we shall say no more about it,' he said through stiff lips. 'I bid you good day, madam!'

Constance rose up with a little pleading gesture. But he had gone.

He had gone and left her, all too late, with the realization that she was in love with him.

Hard on the heels of his departure, Mr Barrington and his wife were announced.

Constance forced a smile of welcome on her face and moved forward to greet them. Mr Barrington was a cadaverous man somewhere in his thirties, with a long, lugubrious face. His wife, by contrast, was small and plump and blonde, with wide, empty, china-blue eyes and an alarming titter.

Mrs Barrington was the first to speak after introductions had been performed. 'La!' she cried. 'Don't you look fine! That silk must have cost all of five shillings a yard, I do declare. Where is the Lady Amelia? Lord, I just pine to catch a glimpse of her!'

Constance explained that Amelia was gone from home and not expected back until late. Mrs Barrington gave a *moue* of disappointment and relapsed into silence, leaving her husband to break into speech.

'And how do we go on?' he asked, after Constance had rung for refreshments. 'Fine feathers make fine birds, Miss Lamberton. "There is an upstart crow beautified with our feathers," heh? Is that one of my lady's gowns?'

Constance pretended not to have heard either the question or its preceding insult and instead burst out, 'Oh, you must help me leave this house, Mr Barrington. I am sure I could work for you. I am not afraid of hard work. My life here is torment. See how Lady Amelia has beaten me!' And she turned her back to show them the weal.

She then clutched his hands and gazed pleadingly into his face.

'Tush! Tush!' said Mr Barrington, trying to disengage himself. 'I have never heard of such ingratitude. But I see what it is. You have to work here as a companion, heh? But you would rather be sitting in comfort in my household and do nothing for your keep.'

Constance flushed angrily under the unjust attack. 'No such thing!' she cried. 'I tell you I am grossly ill-treated here. I am prepared to work for you in any capacity.'

'Here is ingratitude of the worst!' cried Mr Barrington. 'Lady Amelia rescues you from a life of poverty and gives you all this —' here he swept a bony hand in the direction of her dress — 'and yet you wish to run away. Shame on you! And what if you *were* whipped? Why, I whip my own servants if they are lazy.'

To Constance's infinite fury and embarrassment, Mr Barrington sank on to his knees and began to pray in a loud voice. 'Forgive this ungrateful handmaiden, O Lord, so that she may be spared the torments of hell-fire. Look down . . .'

But that was as far as he got. Constance had picked up the teapot and had started to pour a thin stream of scalding tea over his bent head.

He leapt to his feet with a howl of pain. 'Come, Amy!' he cried to his wife who had sat munching cake in an abstracted way through the whole proceedings. 'Let us leave this . . . this . . . *ungrateful* hussy!'

'Oh, aren't I going to meet Lady Amelia, then?' wailed Amy as she was dragged from the room still clutching her cake. 'I shall write to Lady Amelia today,' howled Mr Barrington from the hallway. 'She shall hear of what you said!'

Then the street door banged and Constance collapsed in a chair.

'Fine work you've made of this day,' sneered the voice of Bergen, the butler, from the doorway. 'Turned down my lord and then slandered my mistress to your relatives. Just you wait till my lady gets back!'

'Go away, Bergen,' said Constance in a tired little voice, 'or I shall open that window and tell the whole street of your insolence.'

She seemed in such a wrought-up state and she made a half move to rise from her chair. Bergen believed she might do just that, and he knew the other household servants would support Constance, so he sulkily backed out. He suddenly decided it might be better to let his mistress discover Miss Lamberton's goings-on for herself.

Constance sat trying to control the shaking of her body. What on earth was she to do? After fit punishment had been meted out by Amelia, she would undoubtedly find herself out on the street.

Her only hope now was that Lord Philip

would accept her, after all. When she remembered the furious look of hurt pride on his face, her heart sank. But he was the only person she had to turn to. She would need to visit him at his home. There was no other way. But where did he live?

She rose and stood staring blindly out of the window.

Her eyes suddenly focused on the figure of the Riders' secretary, Mr Evans, who was walking past the house. She ran out into the street, desperately calling after him until he heard her and stopped and walked back to where she was standing.

'Please, Mr Evans!' cried Constance, quite wildly. 'I must find Lord Philip Caultry immediately. Do you know his direction?'

'He lives in Albemarle Street,' said the secretary, surprised. 'I do not know if he will be at home but you could send a footman round with a letter, asking him to call.'

'Oh, no!' said Constance, thinking of the waiting and listening Bergen. 'I must go to his home. Please, will you escort me?'

'I have several commissions to effect for Lady Eleanor . . .' began the secretary doubtfully.

'Oh, *please!*' called Constance, looking frightened out of her wits.

'Very well,' said Mr Evans, thinking rapidly of an excuse to explain his delay to Lady Eleanor — any excuse, that was, but the correct one. Lady Eleanor would not love the idea of him squiring Miss Lamberton to her brother's house.

When Constance had collected her bonnet and shawl, he politely offered his arm and then hailed a passing hack. When they were seated in its smelly interior, he said doubtfully, 'It is not the thing at all for a young lady to call unescorted to a gentleman's home. You appreciate I will have to leave you there?'

'It doesn't matter,' said Constance bravely. 'I am already ruined.'

Anyone else would immediately have wanted to know how the young lady became ruined, but not Mr Evans. He felt he had enough worries in his life at the moment, and did not want to hear about anyone else's. As the hackney drew into Albemarle Street, he noticed, however, that Constance kept scrabbling at her wrist. He hoped she had not got fleas for the hackney carriage was undoubtedly alive with them.

'Is there something up with your wrist, Miss Lamberton?' he asked solicitously as he helped her down from the carriage.

Constance gave a nervous laugh. 'I keep

feeling for my fan,' she said, 'and then I remember I have lost it. It became caught in a rose bush at Lady Eleanor's party.'

'Indeed,' said Mr Evans as he walked up the steps of Lord Cautry's mansion. And then another worry entered his brain. 'Are you sure Lord Philip will wish to see you?'

'I-I think so. I hope so,' said Constance.

Mr Evans decided not to wait. If by any chance Lord Philip was annoyed at the presence of this young lady, then he, Evans, did not want to be around to share his lordship's annoyance.

He accordingly performed a massive tattoo on the knocker, and with a jerky lift of his hat fled off down the street.

Constance was left alone to give her name to a disapproving butler who ushered her into a small salon and shut the door.

She had not long to wait. In a few minutes, the door opened and Lord Philip strode into the room.

He looked handsome and stern and remote. It was hard to believe that this haughty aristocrat had knelt at her feet only a short time before.

'What are you doing here, Miss Lamberton?' he demanded in chilly accents.

Constance made several pitiful efforts to speak and ended by bursting into tears. She felt alone and miserable. How could she have fallen in love with this lord who only considered marrying her a sort of duty? And she suddenly felt sure his pride had been so hurt by her refusal that he would be only too happy to have the chance of refusing *her*.

He made no move to comfort her other than handing her a handkerchief. He stood by the fireplace, his arm leaning against the mantel, and stared coldly down at her, waiting for her to recover.

At last she gave a great gulp and fell silent.

'Go on, Miss Lamberton,' he said.

'I want to marry you, after all,' said Constance.

'Indeed!' he said. He walked across the window and stood with his back to her. It was a very elegant, very unresponsive back.

Constance decided that only the truth would serve . . . the truth except for that one main fact that she had fallen in love with him.

In a halting voice, she began to tell him of the Barringtons' visit and of Bergen's threats.

'And so,' he said icily, without turning round, 'having failed to obtain a post as a governess or a housekeeper in your relatives' home, you consider marriage to me to be the only way out of your predicament.'

'You need not marry me, you know,' said Constance in a small voice. 'I could be a maid in your household or . . .'

He turned round and stared at her haughtily. 'Fustian, Miss Lamberton,' he said. 'I would not consider employing a girl of your family and quality as a maid.'

'Then — as a mistress?' whispered Constance.

'Neither as a mistress.'

'What am I to do?' wailed Constance. Lord Philip stood silent for several minutes staring at her. Her face was slightly blotched with crying, but nonetheless she still managed to look very pretty, fresh and vulnerable. Furthermore, he was tired of his celibate life and fastidiously shrank from the sordid bargaining setting up another ladybird would involve. Children would be splendid to have around. He smiled slowly as he pictured a nursery full of haughty, little high-nosed Cautrys.

'Well, well,' he said briskly, walking towards her. 'Perhaps it would serve after all. I am sure we should rub along together tolerably well. Yes, I will marry you, Miss Lamberton,' said Lord Philip, feeling very magnanimous.

'Oh, thank you,' whispered Constance with true beggar-maid humility, although a

122

nasty, mocking little voice in the back of her brain was evilly pointing out that her beloved Philip was a stuck-up prig.

'Very well,' he said briskly. 'I do not think you should return to Manchester Square. My sister will not, of course, approve of you. She considered your father a trifle wild. I have, however, an elderly aunt living in Brook Street. She does not go out much, but she will take care of you for, let us say, a month until we are married.'

Constance whispered another 'thank you' and he gave her an indulgent smile. His blossoming love for Constance, of which he had as yet been unaware, was being nipped in the bud by the frost of his own splendid magnanimity.

He pressed his cold lips to her forehead and then rang the bell and ordered his carriage to be brought round.

Chapter Eight

Once again, Manchester Square was rent by the infuriated screams of Lady Amelia when the *Gazette* announced the betrothal of Miss Constance Lamberton to Lord Philip Cautry. Once again, Mrs Besant was summoned.

That good lady arrived breathless and exhilarated to view the tantrums and rage of her beautiful friend with indulgent calm.

'You must have been blind, dear Amelia,' said Mrs Besant, carefully laying another log on the bonfire. 'I saw he was enamoured of her long ago.'

'Why didn't you warn me?' raged Amelia, tearing her handkerchief to rags. 'I thought that day she left that she had gone with those relatives of hers, after all. Why didn't Bergen tell me anything? Why didn't you *warn* me . . . or was it because you wanted to hurt me?'

Mrs Besant conjured up a suitably shocked expression on her horse-like face. 'You wrong me, Amelia. You know I am your only friend.' This, at least, was true.

'I could kill her,' grated Amelia. 'I could choke the life out of the little . . .'

'Now, now,' soothed Mrs Besant, feeling quite warm towards Amelia, now that the humiliation had been finally achieved. 'Just you leave things to Mary. I'll think of something . . .'

The Comte Duval turned to his companion, his eyes narrowed into slits. 'Whose fan did you say?'

'Miss Constance Lamberton,' replied the other man proudly.

'You are sure?'

'Course I'm sure. It took a lot of searching and work and . . . er . . . *money* to find out.'

'You will be repaid,' said the comte. 'Where is Miss Lamberton at the moment?'

'She's staying with some old fogey of an aunt of Cautry's in Brook Street. Never goes out. She's going out this evening, however. Cautry's got to take her to dinner at his sister's, Lady Eleanor.'

The comte took out a goose quill and began to ferret among the holes in his teeth while he thought hard. 'For our safety, Miss Lamberton must be removed, although she has said nothing. I must study her again. I feel sure you can engineer an invitation for me for this evening. And also for Miss Braintree. I must use her once more. But that one will not talk. I could ruin Fanny Braintree's reputation for life, and she knows it. She will continue to do what I ask.'

'Pinching papers from her old father's office!'

'That . . . and other things,' smiled the comte.

'Which of us will kill Miss Lamberton?' asked the other uneasily.

'Why me, dear boy,' smiled the comte. 'I and my little wits — I will kill Constance Lamberton.'

Lady Eleanor looked down the long gleaming table to where her brother sat with his fiancée, and her massive bosom heaved.

'It's disgraceful,' she whispered to her husband for the umpteenth time. 'There's bad blood in the Lambertons. They're an old family, I'll admit, but never a title among the lot of them. Disgraceful! This wedding must be stopped.'

'How?' queried her husband with a rare

burst of irritation. 'How will you stop it? By killing the girl?'

'I might,' said his wife grimly. 'I just might!' And for one uneasy moment her husband wondered whether she were joking.

Despite all her ill-wishers Constance appeared to survive. She sat, on the evening before her wedding, in Lady Agatha Beance's drawing-room and tried to fight down an acute bout of premarital nerves. Philip's aunt, Lady Agatha, had been extremely kind. She was a slightly deaf, elderly lady who appeared to have enjoyed Constance's company immensely, having at last found someone willing to read novels to her by the hour. In the past month they had got through the four volumes of *The Rival Mothers* and three of *The Supposed Daughter.*

'If life were like a novel,' thought Constance, 'Philip would have fallen in love with me by now.'

But she had hardly seen her fiancé except for a few carriage drives, and one terrible dinner at the Riders where Lady Eleanor had hissed and fumed at her like an aristocratic volcano all evening.

'He will never fall in love with me now,' thought Constance with a rare burst of insight. 'He's so pleased with himself for taking care of my future that I swear he looks on me in the light of a charity case.'

Lady Agatha lived among the fading glory of the chinoiserie phase of the last century. Constance stared vaguely at the little Chinese men walking over bridges and under willow trees up and down the wallpaper, and wondering with the front of her mind why Chinese artists were so bad when it came to perspective while the rest of her brain scuttled and fretted round the ever present worry. 'Will he ever love me? You cannot love someone you pity. It is better to give than receive, except, of course, life is rather hard if one has been placed in a position always to be the receiver. Is *he* having second thoughts?'

Lord Philip was. No amount of blue blood flowing in his veins, no amount of titles or family crests or family pomp could protect him from that universal illness — premarital nerves.

Constance had been, well, not overwhelmed enough, he decided irritably. On the few occasions he had seen her since his proposal, she had been very quiet and timid and seemed distressingly unaware of his great condescension.

His bachelor life had assumed a rosy and

enchanting glow it never had before.

He was roused from his thoughts by the arrival of Peter Potter who ambled in, in his usual way, unannounced.

He was impeccably dressed as ever but had crowned it all by his usual lapse of memory by having a red Kilmarnock cap pulled down over one ear. He looked for all the world like an extremely gentlemanly pirate.

'You are wearing your nightcap,' said Lord Philip grumpily, and then burst out with what was really worrying him. 'I can't help wishing I didn't have to go through with this wedding tomorrow. Constance does not seem aware of the sacrifice. I could, after all, have looked higher.'

'"Young Adam Cupid, he that shot so trim/When King Cophetua lov'd the beggar-maid",' quoted Peter, 'except in your case, Adam Cupid seems to have missed. I thought you loved the girl.'

'I am very fond of her,' said Philip stiffly.

'Oh, no you're not,' said Peter. 'You're in love with the idea of the high and mighty Philip proposing to the penniless Miss Lamberton. *She* has no high and mighty pride.'

'She's got nothing to be high and mighty about,' snapped Philip, feeling edgy as he again thought of the ceremony on the morrow.

'You're nervous, that's all,' said Peter, pulling off his cap and staring at it for a few seconds in amazement. 'Otherwise I should be deuced angry at you for talking such snobbish fustian.'

'I suppose I am,' sighed Philip with a disarming smile. 'Getting to sound quite like my sister, eh? Oh well, there's nothing can be done about it now.'

'Come round to the Cocoa Tree and have a bumper with me,' said Peter. 'You're as blue-devilled as a monkey's arse.'

Lord Philip grinned. 'For a poet, you have a strange way with words, Peter,' he said with a laugh. 'Yes, I'll go with you, but, dear God, I wish this curst, boring wedding were over and finished with!'

There had been the awkward question of who would give the bride away. The ever efficient Evans had been toped in to help and had come up with an old friend of Constance's father, Squire Benjamin Coates, a bluff and heavyset man who looked ill at ease in his finery, and smelled strongly of the stables.

He was nonetheless a kindly fatherly man who had given away four of his own daughters at the altar, and Constance was grateful for his reassuring presence on the following morning as she was helped into the chariot — or 'charrot', as she had been taught to pronounce it by the ladies of the *ton*.

It was a splendid 'charrot' drawn by satin-skinned chestnuts with silver-plated harness, hung with sumptuous hammer cloths, blazing with armorial bearings. The coachman in the spun-glass wig and pink stockings who sat atop the box was sporting a large nosegay in his buttonhole in honour of the occasion, as did the two huge flunkeys who clung to the back straps.

The sun blazed down with a ferocious yellow, glittering light which to Constance's countrybred eyes meant there was a windy storm shortly to follow. She sat awkwardly in the uncomfortable confines of a French corset which seemed designed to push her bosoms up round her ears. Constance felt her wedding dress was overly fussy with its masses of white silk and lace, all flounced and gored and tucked and ruched and vandyked.

But the waiting, watching crowds of servants along Brook Street who had come out on the steps to see her off found nothing amiss. They thought Constance looked exactly how a bride should look, pretty and fresh and virginal.

Lord Philip when he turned from the altar to watch Constance coming up the aisle on Squire Benjamin's arm was inclined to share their opinion, and felt some new and strange stirrings of pride as he viewed the ethereal vision in white.

The sun slanted in flashes of gold and blue and crimson through the tall, stained-glass windows.

To Constance, Lord Philip seemed like a stranger in the rose silk grandeur of his wedding coat and knee breeches, with jewels flashing on his shoes, his fingers and his cravat.

With a feeling of unreality, she took her place beside him. Peter was best man. There was no maid of honour for Constance, Mr Evans's energies having stopped short at the squire.

The Barringtons were present, since social custom decreed that even the most poisonous of one's relatives must be on the guest list.

Constance made her responses in a low, clear voice, until she was asked whether she would take this man in marriage. She opened and shut her mouth, overcome with a wave of nervous fear, wondering if there was any alternative to marrying a man she loved but who obviously did not love her.

Lord Philip stared down at her in angry embarrassment, and then turned his head away impatiently and stared up at the gallery of the church.

And that is how he noticed the long barrel of a pistol poking over the edge of the gallery, pointing straight at Constance's heart.

In a faltering voice, Constance said, 'I do,' and then everything seemed to happen at once. Lord Philip gave her an almighty push which sent her flying backwards down the aisle as a deafening report rang out. The ball, meant for Constance, hit the squire who had stumbled forward to her aid, and he collapsed like a stone.

Scream after feminine scream rent the congregation as Philip nimbly sprang up the pulpit and leapt from the top of it so that his fingers grasped the brass rail of the gallery. He heaved himself over and then stared wildly around. Nothing. No one.

Down below, the ceremony was in total chaos. Several rowdy bloods at the back of the church who did not know about the shooting thought the whole thing was some mad jest, and began leaping towards the gallery from the top of the pews, cheered on by wild hunting calls from their less agile friends. Every single female in the congregation, with the exception of Constance, seemed to find it an excellent opportunity to prove the aristocratic delicacy of their nerves to the stronger sex, and it seemed as one woman, fainted dead away.

Philip climbed back down the way he had gone up and dropped beside Constance who was being supported by Peter. He pushed roughly past them and knelt beside the fallen squire, opening his waistcoat and feeling for his heart.

Squire Benjamin slowly opened one blue eye and then cautiously opened the other. His broad hand scrabbled inside his coat, and then he began to laugh as he hauled himself to his feet.

'The ball must have bounced off the steel of my demned corset,' he said cheerfully. 'And to think how I cursed when my wife insisted I wear the contraption!'

Constance began to giggle nervously, and Lord Philip's head snapped round and he stared at her with some impatience.

'I really think, my lord,' came the gentle voice of the bishop, 'that we should postpone the rest of the ceremony until another day.'

'Oh, get on with it,' said Philip rudely. He found he was very much shaken. 'I don't want to have to go through this curst ceremony again.' Like the shadow which fell on Constance's face, a cloud covered the sun outside and the church grew dim.

Somehow, the bishop managed to bring order to his unruly flock, and the ceremony went on, Philip angry and worried and Constance white and miserable.

'He didn't want to marry me!' said a nagging voice, over and over again in her brain.

The wedding feast was to be held at Lady Eleanor's Kensington villa. The carriages made their stately way along the Chiswick Road under a now lowering sky. Great gusts of hot wind whirled the dust round in miniature tornados, and the old trees beside the road sighed like the sea as the wind swept through the thick summer foliage.

Constance sat awkwardly in her wedding finery and stole a look at her husband. He was leaning back, his head against the squabs, with his eyes half closed.

Suddenly he opened them and stared at her. 'Who do you think would want to kill you?' he said in a very matter-of-fact voice.

'No one,' said Constance. 'Surely it was some maniac, some radical.'

'Taking potshots at the aristocracy? No, I don't think so,' said Lord Philip and fell silent again.

A sudden squall of rain streamed down the windows of the chariot through which the villas of Kensington danced and wavered as if underwater.

Constance felt the beginnings of anger. Someone had nearly killed her on her wedding day, and yet this brand-new husband of hers had never so much as held her hand or tried in any way to allay her fears.

She bit her lip as she thought of the night ahead. Would he? But of course he would. Memories of Amelia's salacious conversation thudded in her ears and her face burned.

She knew, of course, that it was considered extremely vulgar of ladies and gentlemen of the *ton* to betray the slightest sign of emotion, neither anger, grief, or, it seemed, passion.

Constance reflected that she had been very naive. She had expected that the minute they were married, Lord Philip would immediately change from his aloof self and, well . . . *woo* her.

The marquees were again erected on the lawn, heaving and straining at their guy ropes like tethered elephants.

136

Now, Constance had not drunk any wine since her experience with the Riders' champagne. But she was overcome by the need for some Dutch courage. She had at first been relieved to notice the absence of Lady Amelia, but the green-eyed monster soon reared its ugly head in the shape of a captain's pretty wife, Marjorie Banks-Jyce. She was a pert little brunette with a perfect figure and a roguish, roving eye. Various wives sat and smouldered as she flirted with their husbands, and Constance sat and smouldered with the best of them, particularly when she noticed that Marjorie had succeeded in making her husband smile for the first time that day.

Instead of having one long formal table for the wedding breakfast, Lady Eleanor had had separate little tables arranged around the marquee, with the result that the occasion had turned into a sort of moveable feast with everyone wandering from table to table. As Constance watched narrow-eyed, drinking her fifth glass of burgundy, Lord Philip bestowed a light flirtatious kiss on Mrs Banks-Jyce's wrist and then strolled back towards his wife.

He had a grin on his face and Constance quickly lowered her eyes. She did not know that Philip had just been thinking how pretty his wife looked, and that the Mrs Banks-Jyces of this world were all very well but thank goodness he hadn't married one.

'How is my bride?' he asked in a light, teasing voice.

' "They were as fed horses in the morning; every one neighed after his neighbour's wife",' said Constance bitterly.

'Dear God,' said Philip acidly. 'Only you, dear Constance, would think of quoting Jeremiah on your wedding day.'

'And only you, dear Philip, would think of flirting with another woman on your wedding day,' countered Constance sweetly.

Philip's face was a mask of hauteur. 'Madam, I find you insolent,' he remarked in chilling accents and strode away, only to have his bad temper fanned by Peter Potter who asked him what he thought he was doing, paying court to that Banks-Jyce woman.

'I don't know what's come over you, Peter,' he said, regarding his friend's amiable sheep-like face with irritation. 'In all the years of our friendship, I've never known you to carp and nag as much as you've been doing recently.'

'Never had to,' said Peter, quite unabashed. 'You won't find me standing champion to a lot of Haymarket ware. Those ladybirds were *paid* for their services, after all. I mean, that's pretty much all they expected. You're a fair man with your servants and a good landlord, but up till now you've never really had to consider anyone's feelings but your own.'

'I should not have to concern myself with them in this case,' said Lord Philip. 'She owes me a debt of gratitude. She has no right to twit me on my behaviour. Just look at her now!'

Constance, fortified by a great deal of wine, was attempting to play the flirt with Mr Evans, of all people, and to Lord Philip's fury, the secretary seemed to be enjoying the experience very much.

Lord Philip was about to go and join them when his arm was firmly imprisoned by Squire Benjamin. The squire felt that Lord Philip ought to have the benefit of his advice. After all, he, the squire, was the proud father of four daughters and felt he was qualified to discourse on the gentler sex. Philip could see no way of escape. He allowed Squire Benjamin to draw him aside and then, never once taking his hard, green stare from his wife, he listened to not one word of the good squire's advice.

By the time he escaped, the dancing had commenced. The first dance was a country one, affording him no opportunity to tell Constance how much her behaviour had shocked him. Her pretty face was flushed and her eyes were like stars. Constance was enjoying the novelty of being headily intoxicated and having a great deal of compliments paid to her by the gentlemen guests. She did notice that Philip was glaring at her, but all it did was want to make her giggle.

Lord Philip endured the next hour as Constance flirted and the guests gossiped about the shooting, and sighed with relief when it was time to take his wife away.

He remembered he had told her that they would move immediately to his town house. Now he felt that he really should have taken her somewhere more romantic on their first night together, and the fact that he hadn't suddenly caused him to feel guilty, and the unaccustomed feeling of guilt made him more bad-tempered than ever.

She was waltzing with Peter Potter and laughing helplessly at something that gentleman was saying, and Lord Philip was waiting for the end of the dance impatiently so that he could say goodbye to this curst reception, when, all at once, it seemed as if the gods had taken pity on him at last.

With a great whoosh, a tremendous gust of wind tore the marquee from its moorings and whipped it up and across the garden. Rain swept across the wedding guests, drenching gowns and coats and jewels and feathers, and giving a great proportion of the party the first decent wash they had had in months.

A battalion of footmen soon appeared with umbrellas and rugs, and the soaking guests were huddled into the house to change. Lord Philip caught Constance as she was about to race across the garden.

'Home,' he said grimly.

'I can't go home now,' yelled Constance above the clamour of the storm and the shrieks of the guests. 'I am soaking wet.'

'You can dry yourself at home just as well as you can here,' said Lord Philip. He snapped his fingers and told one of the footmen to have his carriage brought round.

It was a horrendous journey back. Twice it seemed as if the chariot would be hurtled into the ditch, and once the coachman was blown from his box, and although unhurt, was nearly in tears over the damage done to his finery.

Constance had never believed until now that hate could be akin to love. But in that minute she hated Lord Philip who could dismiss the poor coachman's grief as 'tiresome rubbish'.

Constance hardly noticed her new quarters as she allowed herself to be dried and changed by her lady's maid. The lady's maid was French, a grim, silent woman with her hair screwed painfully up on top of her head and snapping black eyes which reminded Constance of the comte. She felt even more furious with her husband, feeling that she should have had some say in hiring her own lady's maid.

Wearing a white muslin dress, its deep flounces decorated with little garlands of artificial flowers — a present from Lady Agatha — Constance surveyed herself critically in the pier glass before going downstairs to join her husband.

She grudgingly admitted to herself that her maid, Bouchard, knew her job well. Her hair had been changed from its usual severe coronet to a rioting mass of curls on top with one heavy soft ringlet falling on to her shoulders.

Lord Philip was waiting for her in his dark and rather sparsely furnished drawing-room. The heavy dark curtains cut off whatever light there was from the stormy day outside. The walls were covered with hunting pictures and various studies of horses. There was no fire burning on the hearth and the floor was bare of rugs. It smelled faintly of dry rot and disuse.

Her lord looked at her enigmatically as she entered and poured her a glass of brandy.

'The coachman, my lord,' said Constance firmly. 'I would like to send a note to the stables assuring him of a new livery.'

Lord Philip looked at her in haughty surprise. 'The one he has will do quite well when it is cleaned.'

'But don't you see,' cried Constance, made courageous by the effects of brandy descending on top of an already wine-filled stomach. 'It means so much to him. It will never look so grand when it is cleaned. Coachmen are very conscious of their appearance, you know. It would quite spoil things for him at the next grand occasion were he not as fine as his fellow coachmen.'

'I am not about to concern myself with the vanities of my coachman . . .' began Lord Philip but was interrupted by a quiet, 'Please,' from Constance.

He surveyed her from under his heavy lids and at last said coldly, 'Very well. You may have your wish.'

He scribbled a note, standing at a desk in the corner. He sanded it and gave it to a footman who ran round to the mews at the back of the house with it. The coachman could not read, so the second footman, a garrulous man considered to be greatly educated, read the contents to him. In the mysterious way of servants, they immediately knew the unexpected kindness was all Constance's doing and the lady's maid, Bouchard, who tried that evening to relate in scornful accents the paucity of my lady's wardrobe was firmly put in her place by no less a personage than Mr Masters, my lord's butler.

Supper was served to the newly-married couple in the dining-room. A stormy night had fallen outside. The couple ate silently, facing each other down the long expanse of mahogany. The room was heavily silent, broken only by the wailing of the wind outside and the occasional jingle of harness as some brave members of the *ton* braved the filthy evening. The candles streamed and flickered, sending little white rivers of wax dripping on to the crystals of the chandelier.

'It was an unusual wedding, my lord,' said Constance at last in a thin voice.

'Quite,' replied her spouse, studying the contents of his plate as if he had just found the mutton guilty of a social gaffe.

'I was very frightened,' added Constance, determined to make some sort of conversation.

'Of course,' replied her lord infuriatingly. 'I have been wondering who attempted to kill you. You didn't leave any broken hearts down in that godforsaken part of the peasantry you hail from? No lovelorn ploughmen sighing in anguish?'

Constance picked up her wineglass, glad to notice her hand was steady, and stared at him over the rim. 'Not I, my lord,' she remarked. 'It is more likely to be some relic of your own highly coloured past than mine.'

'Explain yourself!'

Constance drank the contents of her glass in one gulp. 'I have heard,' she said slowly and distinctly, 'that the members of the corps de ballet at the opera are notoriously hot-headed.'

'A lady never refers to or *notices* her husband's past affairs with the Fashionable Impure,' retorted his lordship, the glitter in his eyes betraying his annoyance.

'Oh, really,' said Constance sweetly. 'But a *gentleman* can, of course, insult his wife by referring to mythical affairs with ploughmen.'

'I married you,' grated Lord Philip, 'because I found your modesty becoming. I am afraid I was mistaken in you.'

'As I was in you,' retorted Constance, her

face flushed with anger. '*I* thought *you* were human. This should have been the happiest day in my life. But instead, I am nearly killed and you go on as if somehow it were all *my* fault. The only affection you have shown all day is towards that little trollop, Marjorie Banks-Jyce.'

Lord Philip dabbed his mouth fastidiously with his napkin. 'You're jealous,' he said.

Constance's hand flew to her glass. She picked it up and threw it full at her husband. He dodged, and it went sailing over his head and struck the door.

As if answering a knock, Masters, the butler, opened the door and entered the room, followed by two footmen, and proceeded to supervise the serving of the pudding as if nothing was amiss.

My lord's and my lady's faces which had a bare moment ago been contorted with anger were now masks of well-bred calm.

'A dreadful evening, is it not?' remarked Lord Philip, stabbing his whipped syllabub to the heart.

'Indeed, yes,' said Constance. 'Very stormy. Quite appropriate, is it not?'

Lord Philip eyed the footman who was sweeping up the broken glass. 'I agree,' he said in a hard mocking voice. 'Love is always stormy, my dear.'

Masters smiled indulgently and heaved a romantic sigh.

'I hope Squire Benjamin will not try to travel home on a night like this,' Constance essayed.

'He will stay in town with my sister. Evans made the arrangements . . . you violent, spiteful, little cat!'

The last remark was made immediately after the door closed behind the servants.

'I was much goaded,' said Constance. She rose to her feet and walked down the length of the table towards the door. 'I shall leave you to your port, my lord.'

He leaned back in his chair and surveyed her as she walked towards him, her face flushed and her bosom heaving. She had never looked more beautiful. He reached out as she passed him and grasped her wrist. He meant to tell her so, but instead found himself saying, 'I shall forego my port, tonight. I think it is time we retired.'

Constance looked down into the glittering green eyes and her courage began to ebb. It had been a false courage after all, wine-induced. She had never before answered back to anyone the way she had answered back to this husband of hers.

Her long eyelashes dropped to veil fear and embarrassment in her eyes.

'Then I shall see you in the morning,' she said in a trembling voice.

He released her wrist. 'You shall see me long before then,' he said. 'But you may go up now and I shall join you shortly.'

Constance trailed miserably from the room. A footman bearing a branch of candles appeared as if by magic, and she followed him upstairs to her room. She dismissed her lady's maid, Bouchard, who gave a sour curtsy and escaped to join the servants' celebration below stairs.

Constance wandered from her sitting-room into the bedroom and stared at the great canopied bed against the wall. She slowly undressed and put on a ridiculously flimsy nightgown. Who had chosen it? Philip?

She felt very young and alone and frightened. Lady Amelia's salacious whispers muttered in her ears like so many demented ghosts.

And then she thought she heard a soft footstep in the corridor outside.

Lord Philip, clad only in an elaborate gold and blue dressing gown, strode into his wife's bedroom. He did not look towards the bed, but marched to the fireplace and moodily stared down at the glowing coals.

Apart from the red light from the fire, the room was in darkness. He was uneasily prey to a series of conflicting emotions. Up till this point, he had naturally considered that his wife would spend their wedding night in his arms. That was the natural way of things. He was in no doubt that she would not enjoy the experience, although he knew himself to be a practised lover. No lady ever enjoyed sex, and it was natural and fitting that she should not. Such base pleasures were only felt by gentlemen, and women of the demimonde and the lower classes.

But a nasty little nagging voice in his brain was telling him that at least he should have tried to woo her. Nonetheless, he must go through with it. It was unthinkable that a man should not bed his own wife. Any other course of action and the planets would reel in their courses, and furthermore, the population of England would decline.

He removed his dressing gown, squared his shoulders and marched up to the bed.

Empty!

He could not believe his eyes. Lord Philip lit a candle beside the bed and held it up. The covers of the bed were turned back but of Constance there was no sign.

He was about to put on his dressing gown and go in search of her when a small stifled sound coming from somewhere quite near made him pause. He held up the candle again, his eyes raking round the silent room. Again, that little noise.

He slowly put the candle back on the table and knelt down on the floor and looked under the bed.

In the red light from the fire, he saw Constance. She was lying under the bed, pressed against the far wall, with a handkerchief pressed against her mouth to stifle her sobs.

She stared at her naked husband, her eyes dilating with terror. Lord Philip Cautry's muscular body had made many a feminine heart beat faster but never before with fear.

'Come out of there,' he said gently. 'Come!'

He stretched out his hand imperiously and Constance allowed herself to be pulled out. Lord Philip retrieved his dressing gown and shrugged himself into it. He indicated a chair at the fireplace.

'Sit down!' he commanded, seating himself opposite as the trembling girl obeyed him. 'Now, my girl, I expect a certain amount of nervousness from a virginal girl, but this is ridiculous. Explain yourself.'

Constance dried her eyes and looked at him bleakly.

'I cannot, my lord,' she said in a low voice, 'bring myself to perform even *one* of the exhausting and humiliating acts expected of me.'

'Fustian,' said her lord, his thin brows snapping together. 'You will soon get used to, what is, after all . . . What exhausting and humiliating acts are you talking about?'

And so Constance told him in a faltering voice all she had learned from Lady Amelia, the words sounding doubly obscene coming as they did from such innocent lips.

Lord Philip felt a faint twinge of regret. Perhaps he should have bedded Amelia, after all. It appeared as if she would have been a highly inventive mistress. But then that was pushed from his brain by a sudden wave of compassion and tenderness for the young wife opposite. He leaned forward and drew her on to his knees, holding her very gently.

'I am truly sorry,' he said in a low voice. 'I had not realized — did not guess — what filth that monster of a woman would have told you. It is not like that at all. It is a matter of love between man and wife.'

'Love!' cried Constance harshly, trying to pull away from him.

'Yes, love — even in this marriage of arrangement,' he said gently, beginning to stroke the long shining tresses of black hair.

Suddenly tired and exhausted with emotion, she leaned against him, only wanting her fear to cease.

He turned her face gently up to his and then bent his head and kissed her very softly and for a long time, until the trembling lips beneath his own began to cling and burn.

When at last he carried her to bed, Constance wound her arms round his neck and buried her head in his chest. She would now have gone with him anywhere, done anything, just so long as he did not stop . . .

Sometime in the small hours of the morning, Lord Philip awoke in the tousled battlefield of his marriage bed. It was cold, and the blankets and sheets appeared to have tied themselves into a Gordian knot at the foot of the bed. He finally wrenched them apart and drew them tenderly over his wife's naked body. She awoke and stared up at him with wide questioning eyes.

And that was when Lord Philip Cautry fell irrevocably in love with his wife. He felt awed and happy and strangely embarrassed as he buried his face in her breast and said in a low voice, *'Je t'aime.'*

'What does that mean?' asked Constance.

'Don't you know French?' he teased. 'It means "I love you".'

Constance held him very close. She was so happy, she thought she might cry.

'I know a little French,' she said. '"L'Empereur" . . . "trahison" . . . "espion",' she murmured lazily.

The body against hers seemed to go very still. 'And where did you learn such interesting words?' said Lord Philip, raising himself on one elbow to look down at her.

Constance racked her sleepy brain, but at first she could not remember. 'I think I heard someone saying them — at your sister's party in Kensington,' she said at last. 'Probably the Comte Duval. He is the only Frenchman I know. Oh, yes — I remember now. He was talking to a friend — an English friend.'

She looked up at him anxiously. In the pale dawn light, his face looked very set and stern.

'You said you loved me, Philip,' she said, stroking his cheek. 'I love you too. I'm afraid I fell in love with you that first night I saw you.'

The green eyes glinted down into her own. Lord Philip traced the line of her swollen lips gently with one long finger.

'Then prove it, Constance,' he said in a teasing voice. 'That is, if you are not too tired . . .'

Chapter Nine

Mrs Mary Besant sourly turned down the corner of her card to show that she had called in person, handed it to her groom to deliver to Lord Cautry's butler, and then ordered her coachman to drive her to Lady Amelia's.

'Four o'clock, my dear,' she cried to Amelia as soon as Bergen, the butler, had retired, 'and they were not even out of *bed!*'

'What do you expect?' snapped Amelia. 'They only got married yesterday.'

'But I thought up such a good idea to embarrass her . . .' began Mrs Besant, but was interrupted by her beautiful friend.

'I'm not interested,' retorted Amelia pettishly. 'They're married and that's that. I never waste my charms on lost causes.'

'But you wanted her dead,' wailed Mary Besant.

'Not any more,' yawned Amelia. 'I have other fish to fry.'

In another part of London, rage against Constance was also dying out. 'I shall just have to make the best of things,' said Lady Eleanor to her husband. 'If I had not given the reception or had stayed away from the wedding, Philip would never have spoken to me again, and family comes before all else. We Cautrys must stick together, and she is now a Cautry.'

'Quite, my dear,' said her husband, signalling wildly with his eyes to Mr Evans to provide him with some excuse to escape.

'But she must be taught as to how to go on,' went on Lady Eleanor. 'She has, after all, not been used to such a grand social position. Yes, yes, I think a little schooling from a woman of the world like myself would not come amiss. What is it, Mr Evans?'

'I have some business papers which require Mr Rider's signature urgently,' said the secretary.

'Oh, very well,' said Lady Eleanor with an imperious wave of her hand. 'You may go to attend to them, Mr Rider, but you stay, Mr Evans. I have some errands I wish you to perform.'

'Really, Eleanor,' bleated her spouse. 'I should think one of the footmen . . .'

'I said I wanted Mr Evans, so Mr Evans shall do it,' said his wife testily. 'I am surprised that you should dare to argue on such a trivial point, sir. I wish you to take a message to Lady Philip, Mr Evans. I shall inform her I shall be calling on her on the morrow. I no longer bear the child any ill will. But then I was always famous for my charitable nature!'

Bouchard, the lady's maid, nipped quickly up the area steps. My lady had not appeared from her bedchamber and Bouchard wished to buy herself a few ribbons. As she reached the corner of the street, she was surprised to hear herself being addressed in her native language, and swung round in surprise. A very elegant gentleman with a thin painted face and snapping black eyes made her a very low bow.

'Good afternoon,' he said again, in French. 'I believe I have the honour to address Mademoiselle Bouchard?'

Bouchard gave a nod of assent.

'You see, I am a friend of the Cautrys,' pursued the gentleman. 'My name is Duval, le Comte Duval.'

Bouchard, highly impressed, sank into a deep curtsy, unmindful of the muddy pavement.

'I heard that one of my countrywomen had taken the position of lady's maid to Lady Philip and I felt obliged to find out if you were well-suited.'

'Indeed, yes, milord,' said Bouchard, highly gratified. Just wait till she told that frosty-faced butler about this!

'But then,' went on the comte smoothly, 'I believe her ladyship has some knowledge of French so that should make you feel more at home.'

'No, milord,' said Bouchard with a superior smile. 'Lady Philip doesn't know a word.'

'Ah, yes, neither she does,' smiled the comte. 'I was thinking of somebody else. Good day, mademoiselle.'

He swept the gratified Bouchard another splendid bow and strolled away.

He need not have worried so unduly about little Constance, he thought. Just as well. The murder of a little companion would not attract such a furor, but the mysterious death of my Lady Philip Cautry most certainly would. Constance was perfectly safe — unless of course she decided to take French lessons . . .

Lord and Lady Philip Cautry lay in bed and watched the evening shadows lengthening across the room. Both were feeling debilitated and hungry. Lord Philip felt he could eat a whole saddle of mutton, but he was still suffering from some guilt over his previous churlish behaviour and did not want to voice such an unromantic need. At last to his relief, Constance said timidly, 'I am very, very hungry, Philip. Perhaps we could . . .'

'Indeed, yes,' he said, smiling down at her. 'I could stay here with you for the rest of my life, but I feel we shall starve to death if we don't eat something.'

Constance sat up and yawned, stretching her arms high above her head. The covers fell from her body, revealing two perfect white breasts to her husband's fascinated gaze.

'Oh, my God, Constance, my sweetheart,' groaned her husband, dragging her down against the length of his body. 'I want you again.'

And that was the mistake which led to the first row.

Both emerged from the highly passionate tussle some time later, exhausted, hungry and nervous.

At last seated again in the dining-room, with her husband looking strangely elegant and remote and facing her down the length of the table, Constance suddenly felt as if she were dining with a stranger.

When the servants had retired, she searched around to make some sort of conversation. 'Have I any money?' she asked at last.

'As much as you like,' yawned her husband. 'Why?'

'I am badly in need of some new clothes,' said Constance.

His eyes mocked her. 'I much prefer you without clothes,' he teased and then looked with surprise and some irritation at the painful blush spreading up his wife's neck and face. He did not realize that despite her experience of the bedroom, Constance was still very shy out of it. He was feeling overtired and his nerves were on edge.

'You had better let me choose clothes for you,' he added.

'I shall choose my own clothes,' said Constance with a half laugh, for surely he must be joking.

'Nonsense,' said Lord Philip. 'You are no longer a companion but a lady of fashion, and must dress accordingly. You have not had the necessary experience in choosing dresses suitable for the *ton*. I shall advise you.'

'You'll *what?*' said his wife, her eyes

blazing. Constance was also feeling exhausted and nervy. 'And where did you gain your experience of women's clothes, my lord? In the brothels of Covent Garden?'

'It is as well there is a table between us, or I would give you the smacking you deserve for that piece of cheap impertinence,' said Lord Philip.

'You! Smack *me!* How dare you, sirrah!' gasped Constance.

At this interesting point, the door opened, and Masters the butler appeared with his retinue of footmen and started to serve the next course.

The newly marrieds smouldered at each other down the length of the table until the servants had retired.

'I think,' said Lord Philip haughtily, 'we should forget the previous conversation and pretend it never took place. It was very ill-bred of you . . . Oh, what is it now, Masters?'

'A letter for my lady,' said the butler, presenting it to Constance.

He then retired again from the room as Constance broke open the seal. 'It is from your sister! Let me see . . . wishes to call on me tomorrow . . . feels it incumbent on her to advise me as to the proper behaviour for a Cautry.' Her eyes grew quite round as she read on. 'One springing from such a lowly position as myself should . . . Impertinence!' raged Constance.

Now Lord Philip thought it a prime piece of impertinence himself, but his sister had only been repeating, in a way, what he had just said himself. 'Well, you can't really blame her . . .' he began, unforgivably.

'To think that I ever let you *touch* me!' raged Constance. 'Your mind is as starched as your cravat.' And before he had time to reply, she ran sobbing from the room.

Lord Philip took a hearty swallow of wine and then stared moodily at the decanter. Such emotional scenes were disgracefully ill-bred. No, he would not apologize. He fuelled his bad temper with a few more glasses of wine, unfairly accused Masters of watering it, howled for his carriage and slammed out of the house.

He sat in his curricle and stared at the swishing tails of his horses. He was one of the few aristocrats in London who did not have the tails of his horses docked, considering the process which involved the amputation of several vertebrae in the tail and the searing of the bleeding stump with a hot iron, an inhuman practice. It was almost dark, and already the flambeaux were flaring and smoking outside the neighbouring mansions.

A nagging feeling of guilt tormented him and made him even angrier. Thinking of Constance, he suddenly remembered scraps of the Comte Duval's conversation she had overheard at his sister's.

He remembered how the comte had been courting Fanny Braintree. His anger had found a refreshingly new direction. He set his horses in motion and headed towards Whitehall to consult a certain gentleman at the Foreign Office.

It was two in the morning before Lord Philip arrived home. It had been a stormy meeting. Fanny Braintree and her choleric father, the General, had been summoned to the Foreign Office. Fanny Braintree had wept and fainted, and recovered and wept and fainted again. She had not given any information to the Comte Duval, she had insisted, terrified that her father and these austere gentlemen should find out that she had parted with her virginity as well as her papa's state secrets. The General, at last convinced of his daughter's innocence, had led her away. Fanny was to be sent off to relatives in Scotland, however, to remove her from the dangerous comte's notice.

Lord Philip was commissioned to keep a close watch on the comte. He was not to tell

162

anyone of his suspicions, even his wife. Philip had demurred at this. Surely it would be all right if Constance knew. But the severe gentlemen of the Foreign Office firmly believed all women to be born tattletales. Lord Philip's duty to his country must come first.

He wearily climbed the stairs to his wife's bedroom. The door was locked. He was too tired to feel the slightest twinge of anger, and removed himself to his own rooms to sink into a long and dreamless sleep.

Constance waited, sitting up in bed and staring at the door, hoping one minute that he would go away and the next, that he would try to force the door. As the silence lengthened and she realized he was not coming back, she too fell asleep and dreamed of being hunted across endless muddy fields by Lady Amelia and Mrs Besant.

Despite his exhaustion, Philip woke early — early for London Society, that is — at two in the afternoon. He remembered Amelia was giving a party that afternoon, and decided to attend so that he could begin to study the comte and perhaps discover the name of his English accomplice.

He was informed his wife had not yet

come downstairs. He scribbled her a letter, ate a hasty breakfast, and made his way to Manchester Square. Still tired after his amourous labours of the day before, he did not yet miss Constance, and almost persuaded himself that he had behaved very well indeed.

Constance appeared in the morning-room about ten minutes after his departure and read the letter that Masters handed her.

'Dear Constance,' she read, *'I regret I have a social engagement at Lady Godolphin's this afternoon. You may buy a new wardrobe and tell the dressmakers to send their bills to me. P.'*

No word of love. The letter that Lord Philip had thought magnanimous in the extreme was ripped to shreds. That he should leave her so soon to go dance attendance on Lady Amelia was well nigh past bearing.

Constance was roused from her fury by a discreet cough from the doorway. 'Excuse me, my lady,' said Masters. 'Lady Eleanor has called.'

'Tell her I am not at home,' snapped Constance.

'Very good, my lady,' said Masters.

Constance crossed to the window and observed with satisfaction the angry flush on Lady Eleanor's face as her groom returned from the doorstep to the carriage with the tidings that Lady Philip was not at home.

Lady Eleanor sourly turned down her calling card and handed it to the groom, who returned to the house to give it to the butler. Then he was called back by Lady Eleanor who substituted it with another card with the corner unbent. Lady Eleanor had obviously decided she did not want the upstart Lady Philip to know that she had called in person.

Her carriage rolled off and Constance turned from the window feeling rather flat.

Well, she would go shopping and entertain herself by buying a pretty wardrobe. *Then* her haughty, overbearing husband would find she had excellent taste.

Then Constance bit her lip. She would have to have *someone* in attendance and she did not wish to spoil her day by taking the sour-faced Bouchard with her. She decided to take the more congenial company of one of the footmen and rang for the carriage to be brought round. She was vaguely aware that her husband kept more than one carriage. She did not realize he kept seven.

Constance was soon dreamily lost in a magic world of silks and muslins and beads and feathers and bonnets. The sun was setting by the time the last of her parcels was handed into the carriage.

It was then that she spied the familiar figure of Mr Evans and cheerfully hailed him. Mr Evans seemed delighted to be recognized by the new Lady Philip. He accepted a place in Constance's carriage. In reply to her offer to transport him to wherever he was bound, he said shyly that he had a message to deliver to one of Lady Amelia Godolphin's guests.

Constance had forgotten her rage at Philip and cheerfully agreed to take the secretary to Manchester Square. After all, such a passionate husband would surely be immune to Lady Amelia's charms.

She prattled on absentmindedly about her purchases and then said, 'I am exceeding grand now, Mr Evans. I even have a French lady's maid, although I shall have to take French lessons, I fear. It is not good *ton* to be ignorant of the language, even though we are at war with the country.'

'I think it quite unnecessary,' said Mr Evans. 'No one wishes to speak French these days, Lady Philip.'

Like all shy people who are beginning to emerge from their shell for the first time, Constance became unaccountably stubborn.

'But I should like to learn French very much indeed,' she countered. 'I shall ask my husband to hire a tutor for me.'

Mr Evans grew quite heated, 'I am surprised at you, my lady,' he exclaimed. 'That monster, Napoleon Bonaparte, plans to defeat England. Our men are dying under the sabres of his soldiers. I would not speak one word of their accursed language!'

But Constance was not paying any attention. The carriage had come to a halt in front of Lady Amelia's house in Manchester Square. Candles had already been lit in the downstairs salon and the curtains had not yet been drawn. Close by the window stood Constance's husband. Lady Amelia was smiling up at him and, even as Constance watched, she put a possessive little hand on his sleeve. Bergen, the butler, stood on the step, watching Constance with scarcely concealed hate. She shrank back against the squabs.

'Goodbye, Mr Evans,' she said quietly.

Mr Evans had been staring at the fascinating tableau presented by Lord Philip and Lady Amelia. He hurriedly made his goodbyes after pressing Constance's hand with a warm gesture of sympathy which brought tears to her eyes.

Lord Philip Cautry had not seen his wife's carriage outside the slim mansion in

Manchester Square, but Lady Amelia had. She did not want to waste any more time wooing a lost cause like Lord Philip, but she had to admit it gave her a delicious feeling of power to notice the stricken look on Constance's face. Also, her flirting with Lord Philip annoyed Mary Besant.

Mary Besant was feeling obscurely disappointed in Lord Philip Cautry. She would never have believed that he would have left his wife's arms so soon.

The Comte Duval watched the comedy of manners from his corner of the room. A disappointed wife could be a useful wife, he thought. And Lord Philip had important friends at the Foreign Office. A jealous and bitter wife might be ready to listen closely to her husband's conversations with important men.

Wellesley's repeated victories in the Peninsula were shaking the French Empire to the very core. He had begged to return to his beloved France but his directive was always the same. He must remain in England. The Emperor would need friends on this side of the Channel when he finally overthrew the British and marched his soldiers through St James's.

Duval mulled over Constance's lack of French. The attempt to kill her at her wedding had been a foolish risk. The girl suspected nothing. Had she done so, she would surely have confided in her husband. Or would she? thought the comte studying Amelia and Lord Philip. Lord Philip had held the comte in conversation earlier in the evening, practically gloating over Wellesley's victories and the fact that the Prince Regent had made that infuriating thorn in Napoleon's flesh an Earl. The comte had smiled and agreed to everything, wondering at one point whether Lord Philip were deliberately trying to annoy him.

Lord Philip was suddenly missing Constance desperately. The hour was more advanced than he had realized. He hurriedly took his leave and rushed home, only to find that his wife had left for the opera accompanied by Peter Potter.

He glanced at the clock. They would soon be home. He rang for the brandy decanter and then stretched out his legs and prepared to await their return. But he was still very tired, and in no time at all he was asleep.

And so it was, later that evening, that Constance, emboldened by an enjoyable visit to the opera where she had received a great deal of compliments, and by a longing for the arms of her husband, walked up to his rooms only to find his bed empty.

She lay awake for most of the night, torturing herself with visions of Amelia in Philip's arms. Once again, Amelia's salacious conversation pounded in her ears until poor Constance decided that her own lovemaking had been too naive and innocent to hold an experienced man like her husband. As a brassy dawn rose over the streets of London, she turned her white face into the pillow and cried herself to sleep.

Chapter Ten

Lord Philip awoke the next morning, stiff and hot. The English weather, which had been unseasonably cold and blustery for the past few days, had suddenly decided to become tropical. The air in the drawing-room was already stifling. He felt sweaty, dirty and ill-used. Surely to God his wife's duty was to at least *ask* about him when she came home from entertaining herself at the opera with his best friend. And what of the servants? What the hell had been up with them that they should let their master snore in a hard chair all night?

Masters, when questioned, was at a loss for an answer. The fact was he had ordered the servants not to intrude too much on the newlyweds' happiness and only to go into a room if directly summoned. Now faced with his master's grim and unshaven face, it seemed a peculiarly silly excuse.

After he had breakfast and been barbered, Lord Philip began to feel a trifle better. He sent a footman in search of his wife. When Constance at last entered the room, it was with some irritation that he noticed that she was dressed to go out. Not only that, but her new walking dress of *peau de soie* sported a ridiculous ruffle at the neck and her bonnet, which prettily shadowed her face, was a miracle of the milliner's art, being at least a foot high and embellished at the side with two osprey feathers. She looked very smart and dashing, and Lord Philip would have been the first to appreciate the ensemble on any female other than his wife. As it was, he felt she was making herself unreasonably conspicuous. And so he told her.

And Constance, who had nourished dreams of her husband's eyes lighting up with pride and love when he saw the transfiguration, felt furious and humiliated.

But she showed her hurt feelings by remaining icily calm and dignified, listening patiently to her husband's tirade with a weary smile pinned to her mouth.

'If you have quite finished,' she said at last, 'I have several duty calls to make.'

Now Lord Philip badly wanted to haul his wife off to bed that very minute, and had she shown one sign of softness or affection, he would have done just that. But he felt humiliated because the intensity of his desire was not reciprocated — not knowing that this intensity was manifesting itself in a very arrogant and bad-tempered expression on his face. So he merely made her a very stately bow which Constance replied to with a deep, court curtsy.

Lord Philip watched his wife leave and then decided that action was the only thing to reduce the pain of rejection that he felt. He would go and find Peter and put on the gloves in Gentleman Jackson's Boxing Salon for a few rounds, and then he would continue his pursuit of the Comte Duval. If he could at least discover the identity of the comte's friend — the English traitor — then he would feel he had achieved something.

Constance alighted from her carriage and stared gloomily at Lady Eleanor's house. Duty demanded that she return the call. To her delight, her groom returned to say that Lady Eleanor was at the Kensington villa. So all I have to do is call on that horrible Besant woman, thought Constance.

Her face lit up in a smile as she saw Mr Evans walking down the steps towards the carriage.

'How is Lord Philip?' asked Mr Evans, after bending over her hand.

A shadow crossed Constance's face. 'Well,' she said curtly.

'And what are we doing today?' demanded Mr Evans. 'Is my lady taking French lessons?'

Constance felt the secretary was being a trifle forward but she was nonetheless fond of this quiet, unassuming man so she said the first thing that came into her head to cover her irritation. 'Oh, I shall soon,' she laughed. 'If only to find out the meaning of things like "espion" and "trahison". Now, what have I said, Mr Evans?' An awful thought struck her. 'Oh, dear! They are not *oaths*, I trust?'

'I am afraid they are indeed,' said Mr Evans primly. 'I told you you would be well advised to leave that accursed language alone!'

'Indeed!' replied Constance in a chilly little voice. "What *is* there about me," she thought crossly, "that positively encourages people to tell me what to do and what not to do?" 'You must excuse me Mr Evans. I must call on Mrs Besant.'

The carriage moved off, leaving the secretary standing in the middle of the road, staring after it.

Mrs Mary Besant was unfortunately at home. Thanking the social laws for limiting duty calls to only ten minutes, Constance resigned herself to China tea and English malice.

'I am *so* glad you called, dear Lady Philip. Oh, how *formal* we are,' shrieked Mrs Besant. 'As if I didn't know you when you were nothing but a little waif from the country. I shall call you Constance and you shall call me Mary, and we shall be devoted friends.'

'Quite,' said Constance, feeling thoroughly embarrassed. Time is a peculiar beast. If one is having a perfectly miserable and humiliating time, then the seconds crawl and cough their way round the clockface. Constance stared at an ugly marble clock on the mantel and wondered if it had stopped.

'And you have become such a young lady of the world, so quickly,' gushed Mrs Besant, snapping up saffron cakes with her great yellow teeth. 'To turn a blind eye when Lord Philip flirts with Lady Amelia is very wise, very wise indeed. Husbands cannot bear a jealous woman, you know.'

'What an . . . er . . . interesting house you have,' said Constance in a flat voice, completely ignoring the previous remark. In truth, Constance thought Mrs Besant's home horrible. It looked like a furniture warehouse, since Mrs Besant could never bear to throw anything away. Ugly William and Mary gate-legged tables squatted beside delicate Chippendale chairs. China vases of Dynasty Staffordshire held bunches of wilting flowers. The pictures on the walls were so black and dirty that they looked like framed treacle toffee, and a multitude of greenish mirrors doubled the clutter of the room. Dust motes swam in the pale yellow light of the hot afternoon and a trapped bee buzzed his desire for escape, echoing the frantic desire for escape in Constance herself.

'I often receive compliments on my house,' said Mrs Besant, smugly proceeding to recite a long list of them. 'I don't believe in these modern fads — all this Egyptian nonsense. Give me a comfortable sofa with a back to it, I always say,' said Mrs Besant, complacently slapping the arm of an over-stuffed monster and sending a little cloud of dust up into the somnolent air. 'Now, you must tell me all about your marriage. How does it feel to be a bride?'

The question was innocent in content but almost leering in its delivery as Mrs Besant leaned forward, all teeth and eyes, as if ready to swallow up the secrets of Constance's marriage bed.

The marble clock gave a little sigh and reluctantly choked out the hour. Constance leapt to her feet.

'Thank you for an interesting visit, Mrs Besant,' she said, nervously tugging at the satin ribbons of her reticule.

Mrs Besant looked at her in a baffled way. There was no way she could keep a guest after the regulation ten minutes was up, so with a reluctant sigh, very like that of the marble clock, she allowed Constance to escape.

Constance climbed into her carriage and leaned back in relief. To her surprise, she saw Mr Evans peering in the open window.

'Mr Evans!' she exclaimed. 'How nice to see you again. Can I set you down anywhere?'

'I would indeed be grateful,' said the secretary, climbing into the carriage with alacrity. 'It is uncommon hot. Could you possibly set me down at Mr Rider's.'

Constance gave the instructions to the coachman. She had a sudden longing to get out of London, away from the smell and the press of the traffic and into the cool, green quiet of the country — with Philip, of course, she thought with a sudden painful lurch of the heart. 'I believe if I had put my arms around him this morning,' she thought miserably, 'then everything would have been all right. If I am so jealous of him with Lady Amelia, could he then not be jealous of me going to the opera with Peter?'

She was so engrossed in this novel thought that she failed to notice the secretary's strange nervousness and only looked up in surprise when the carriage stopped outside the Riders' mansion.

'Please allow me to offer you some refreshment,' begged Mr Evans. He saw the hesitation on Constance's face. 'I know it is forward of me,' he added in a low voice, 'but I am of good family, you know, but my low station in life and my lack of fortune often bar me from the conversation of intelligent women of the world. I feel you understand how it is — to be always patronized.'

Yes, Constance did know, and her kind heart was touched. Having little acquaintance in London, she had no further calls to make. Philip's aunt, Lady Agatha, had removed to Brighton. Also, if she rushed home right away, it would probably be to find her infuriating husband absent. Did he indeed spend the night with Lady Amelia? She was so tortured, again with this anguished thought, that she followed Mr Evans into the house, almost blindly.

She roused herself from her thoughts at last to notice that Mr Evans was ushering her into a small, book-lined study. 'I shall fetch the refreshments myself, Lady Philip,' he said. 'The servants are all mostly at the villa in Kensington, and the ones here have been allowed the day off.'

As he went off in search of refreshments, Constance sat down, feeling suddenly ill at ease. It was wrong, she knew, to be sitting alone with this secretary in a house empty of servants. For the first time she wished she had brought her maid, Bouchard. She would stay but a few minutes and then leave.

Mr Evans came bustling in with a decanter and glasses. 'I would prefer tea,' said Constance. 'It is a trifle too warm to be drinking wine.'

Mr Evans stood on one foot and then the other, looking for all the world like a bewildered crane. 'The kitchens,' he bleated feebly. 'Alas! I do not know my way about the kitchens. I fear . . .'

'Never mind,' said Constance. 'Wine will do.'

This visit is definitely a mistake, thought Constance. The room was unbearably warm. She took a sip of her wine and wrinkled her nose. The wine was very heavy and warm and tasted almost medicinal. She chatted resolutely of this and that to the now strangely silent secretary, and at last gathered up her reticule and parasol, preparatory to taking her leave.

'You have not finished your wine,' said Mr Evans.

Constance was about to protest that she did not want any more wine, but a lot of the old Constance — shy, irresolute and timid — had come back.

So, to save argument, she downed the remainder of the glass in one gulp, dropped a demure curtsy, and found she could not rise. Something seemed to have happened to her legs. She stared up at Mr Evans with swimming eyes. The books on the shelves began to swim round and round in front of her eyes, going faster and faster until they became a blur. She stretched up a hand appealingly, gave a faint sound between a whimper and a moan and collapsed senseless on the floor.

Mr Evans stood looking down at her. Her face was very white and covered in sweat. He touched the bell.

Lady Amelia's butler, Bergen, and Constance's lady's maid, Bouchard, came into the room and stood staring at the unconscious girl on the floor.

The secretary turned on them and said in a sharp voice which would have astounded his employers: 'Now you know your part. You are being highly paid to keep your mouths shut. When you have done your job, you will stay in your respective employ for four weeks, and then you will both give notice and leave. You are being paid never to return to London again. Bouchard — you will dress yourself in Lady Philip's clothes. Return to her home, masquerading as her ladyship. Make sure none of the servants sees your face. Lock yourself in her room and when it is dark make your escape to your own quarters. Bergen, after dark, Bouchard will let you in by the side door. You are to rob Lord Philip's jewel box. That is your part. You will keep the jewels as your payment.'

'And what if his lordship returns?' said Bouchard.

'Arrangements have been made to keep Lord Philip away until late,' said Mr Evans.

'Who's behind this?' queried Bouchard suspiciously.

'It's none of your business,' snapped Evans. 'The less you know the better for your own safety.'

He averted his eyes as Bouchard stooped and began to undress the still body. He then noticed Bergen watching avidly. 'Come out of the room until she has finished,' he said, drawing the butler out of the door.

'What becomes of her?' asked Bergen, licking his pale lips.

'That is none of your affair,' said Evans haughtily. He felt suddenly like a general. He felt more important than he had ever done in his life before.

Bouchard eventually appeared from the study and joined the two men. Constance's frivolous bonnet concealed most of the maid's face. The dress was a trifle tight at the seams and short at the ankle, but it would have to do.

'Hold the parasol over your face and *don't talk*,' said Evans. 'I will give instructions to the coachman.'

When the Cautry carriage had rolled off, Mr Evans returned to the silent house. He stared down at the unconscious girl, relieved to notice she was still breathing. He had been afraid he had put too much chloral in the wine. He sat looking at her for a long time, suddenly wondering what to do.

Although it was still early evening when he returned home, Lord Philip Cautry was extremely angry to learn that his wife was lying down with the headache. He rattled the door of her bedroom and called her name several times but only silence greeted him and the door was locked. 'Sulk as much as you like, madam,' he called through the door. 'I have to go urgently to my sister's villa in Kensington. But if this door is still locked when I return, I shall break it down.'

And Bouchard, crouched on the other side of the door, now back in her own clothes, gave a sigh of relief as she heard his angry footsteps clattering back down the stairs.

Mr Evans wearily opened the side door of Lady Eleanor's town house. The Comte Duval slipped in as quietly as a shadow.

'Have you done it?' he asked eagerly.

'Yes,' whispered Mr Evans, his white face gleaming in the dark.

'What did you do with the body?' hissed the comte.

'Tied stones to it and threw it over Westminster Bridge. Nobody saw me. Lady Philip sank down into the water, and the last I saw was her white, white face staring up at me as if begging for help,' shuddered Evans.

'It's the Welsh in you,' said the comte with a laugh, 'all that poetic imagining. You have done well. France is proud of you.'

'That's nice,' said Mr Evans dully. 'That's very nice indeed!'

Chapter Eleven

Seven days had passed since the disappearance of Lady Philip Cautry. The servants had been told not to breathe a word of it, but servants are only human, and after each one had confided in his or her closest friend, and the closest friend had confided in his or her closest friend, soon the whole of the top ten thousand knew that Constance had absconded with her husband's jewels, and gleefully pointed out there had always been bad blood in the Lambertons.

Lady Amelia gave a party to celebrate. Mrs Besant who claimed to have inside information dined out more grandly than she had for some time. Only Lady Eleanor, strangely enough, maintained stoutly that she did not believe a word of it. Philip had gone through the week in a numb daze. He did not want to believe it but what else could he do? Mr Evans, whom he trusted

185

absolutely, had assured him that Lady Philip had been strangely nervous and upset when he had last seen her — so much so that he had felt it his duty to insist she have some refreshment.

Masters, the butler, said that her ladyship had run past in the hall and had stumbled several times as she had climbed the stairs.

When he himself had returned home after a strange summons to his sister in Kensington, and had found his wife missing, he had bad-temperedly assumed she had gone to the opera again, and had gone to his room to change into his evening clothes, only to find his jewel box lying on the floor and most of the contents gone.

A hurried search of his wife's room had revealed that several dresses and a trunk were missing, although the dress and bonnet she had worn that day were lying on the bed.

The most damning evidence was that of the lady's maid, Bouchard. My lady, she had said, had muttered something about not being able to bear it any longer, and had locked herself in her rooms after telling Bouchard to take the rest of the day off.

Mrs Besant had described Constance as 'strange and wild-eyed'. Lord Philip began to think he had not known Constance at all. He had ridden to see her impossible relatives, the Barringtons, but they had not heard from her. He had travelled to Berry House, only to find it deserted and abandoned. It was then that he learned his friend Peter Potter was gone from Town, and no one knew where.

Lord Philip, who had by now wildly conjured up an image of Constance as a wily and cunning seductress, felt quite sure his friend had been dragged into the plot by her. He felt bitterly humiliated.

Peter and his wife . . .

And having felt that he had discovered the reason for Constance's flight, he plunged bitterly into all his old familiar sports and pastimes.

By the second week of Constance's disappearance, London Society had found something else to talk about. Lord Philip did not even know that the urgent note summoning him to go to his sister's in Kensington that night had been a forgery. He had arrived at the villa and had said abruptly, 'I believe you wished to see me on some urgent matter?' And Lady Eleanor, who considered all of her business urgent, had found nothing amiss, and had proceeded to bore him with a long dissertation on how she hoped to get Mr Rider elected to Parliament.

He loved Constance, and he hated her. At

times he prayed he would never see her again so that he could get over his pain, and at others he longed to hold her in his arms so that he could choke the life out of her.

He barricaded his feelings behind a facade of impeccable dress and chilly manners. He had his long hair cut short in the new Brutus crop, and broke more hearts than he had ever done before.

But time did not ease his hurt. It only built up a picture in his mind of a leering, cunning, laughing Constance who had stolen his jewels and his heart and his best friend.

He was dressing one afternoon to go out. It was now four weeks since the disappearance of his wife and he was carefully 'putting on his armour', as his valet sadly described it to Masters. Cravat tied in the Mathematical, coat of Bath superfine, striped waistcoat, doeskin trousers moulded to his long legs, and glossy Hessians, so brilliant that if he stared at his toes he could see the distorted reflection of his white and bitter face.

His valet was flicking a brush across his shoulders when Masters appeared in the doorway of his dressing-room.

'Mr Potter has called, my lord,' said Masters, his face like wood. For the servants had learned from Mr Potter's servants that Mr Potter had disappeared on the night of my lady's disappearance, and had put one and one together, making two.

'*What!*' Lord Philip swung around so violently that he struck the brush from the valet's hand.

'Mr Potter, my lord,' repeated Masters.

Lord Philip took a deep breath.

He strode from the room and slowly descended the stairs.

Peter was sitting in the dark drawing-room, happily sipping Madeira and turning the glass round and round in his fingers. He was busy composing a poem while he waited and was suddenly brought forcibly back to the present as the point of a sword pressed into his neck. He stared up, looking more foolish and sheepish than ever, along a yard of cold steel to the blazing green eyes of Lord Philip Cautry.

'*Where is my wife?*'

Peter blinked, and gingerly took the steel between finger and thumb and tried to push it away.

'I don't know,' he said vaguely. 'I've only just got back. Are you trying to kill me, Philip?'

'I will, an' you don't tell me the doxy's whereabouts,' grated Lord Philip.

'Steady on,' said Peter, feeling the point of the rapier scraping his neck. 'I don't *know.*'

'Where have you been?'

'At Channelhurst,' said Peter. 'My aunt died, you know, the one I told you about. Left me a packet. What on earth is up with you?'

Philip lowered the sword, feeling suddenly weary. As he stared down at his friend's amiable face, he wondered how he could possibly believe Peter guilty of any treachery.

'I must be going mad,' he cried, sitting down in the chair opposite. In a low voice, he told Peter what had happened.

Peter took out his quizzing glass, and began to poke it inside one of his shoes. Then he took the straps of his pantaloons, and began to tug at them one after the other until one of them snapped, and his trouser leg, released from its mooring, began to slowly climb up his leg, revealing a canary yellow stocking embroidered with a bird of paradise.

'You *are* going mad,' he said at last. 'It's *Constance,* we're talking about. Sweetest little girl I ever met. She couldn't do a thing like that. Why should she? She had all the money in the world as Lady Philip.'

'I thought she had gone off with you,' exclaimed Philip. 'God, what a fool . . .'

'Off with me?' Peter's mouth fell open, and he finally closed it again by shoving the knob of his cane under his chin.

'Yes, you. I thought perhaps . . . well, I was very fond of her father, but there's no denying the Lambertons are a wild lot, and . . .'

'You've got windmills in your head. When it comes to that old family name of yours, Philip, you become a different person. You're much too high in the instep for your own good. You're still *ashamed* of having married Constance because you might have had a duke's daughter. Come, now. Admit it! Didn't it ever cross your mind that something might have happened to her? Someone might have been getting money out of her for some reason? After all, someone did try to kill her on her wedding day . . .'

Philip suddenly remembered the Comte Duval, and despite his promises of secrecy to the gentlemen of the Foreign Office, decided he must tell Peter.

'So you see,' ended Philip, 'it was pretty fishy. She only caught bits of it but she remembered "trahison" and "espion" — traitor and spy. The comte and his friend may have thought she understood what was said and was going to blab about it some time or t'other.'

'Well, now you think about it, he may have

been behind her disappearance, so what do we do?' said Peter, sitting up.

Lord Philip gave a nasty smile. 'Why,' he said gently, 'we will do what I should have done a long time ago. We shall go round and pay a call on the Comte Duval — and if he has any information at all, we shall choke it out of him.'

The comte lived in a narrow house in Half Moon Street. Lord Philip and Peter noticed with sinking hearts that the knocker was off the door and the blinds were drawn. The day was slightly chilly, and a small red sun peered through a haze of smokey cloud high above the city. A Punch and Judy man was entertaining a group of servants at the end of the street, and the shrill voice of Judy berating Punch cackled over the cobblestones. At the other end of the street, out of sight, a barrel organ was murdering the music of the young Rossini.

The pair gloomily surveyed the house, and Philip was about to turn away when his eye caught the twitch of a blind on one of the upper floors.

He whispered something to Peter who nodded, and then they walked off down the street.

Through a chink in the blind, the Comte

Duval watched them go. He had known the game was up when he had been seated next to Sir Augustus Curtis at dinner last night. Sir Augustus Curtis was a prominent member of the Foreign Office. He had barely been able to bring himself to speak to the comte, and at one point during the dinner, when the comte had teasingly laid a hand on Sir Augustus's arm, that gentleman had jerked his arm away, and had carefully dusted his sleeve with his lace handkerchief as if the very touch of the comte was contaminating. So they suspected him. They certainly had no proof. But it was time to leave. He had dismissed all his servants, sold his carriages and horses at Tattersall's, and put his property up for sale at Garroway's coffee house in the City. A small portmanteau, his only luggage, lay strapped on the floor. He would wait a few minutes to make sure that accursed pair had well and truly left, and then take a hack to Ludgate Hill and then from there travel by stagecoach to the coast.

He crept quietly downstairs through the deserted empty house and stood behind the front door. Punch's squeaky voice at one end of the street mingled with the strains of *The Italian Girl in Algiers* from the other.

Rapid footsteps approached the house and he waited, holding his breath, only to let it out in a gasp of relief as the footsteps went on past the house.

He cautiously opened the front door a crack, and then stared down at the reflection of his face in a glossy Hessian boot which had been thrust into the crack in the door.

In the next minute Lord Philip Cautry had forced his way in, followed by Peter Potter.

The comte backed off up the shadowy hall, a smile pasted on his thin rouged lips. 'Ah, it is only you, Cautry,' he said, pleased to note that his voice was steady. 'I thought footpads had found their way in.'

'Where's Constance?' said Philip in a cool pleasant voice, which was somehow more frightening than if he had screamed.

'Your wife? Why should I know the whereabouts of your wife?' smiled the comte. 'Come, man, relax and have some wine with me. Your family tragedy has turned your head.'

Philip looked at him. 'Constance overheard you talking to someone at my sister's. No, she didn't know French, but she memorized some of the words and caught the words "traitor" and "spy".'

'Of course she did,' laughed the comte, very much at his ease. 'I was discussing the sad business of traitorous spies working in this country for Napoleon Bonaparte.'

Philip felt his heart sink. Then to his surprise, he heard Peter saying in a light voice, 'Oh, really, my dear comte. Fanny Braintree told us *all*. We know everything down to the last document she stole from her father's desk.'

'Lies,' said the comte weakly, but Philip noticed his face had gone chalky white under his paint.

Surprising both men, the comte darted for the stairs and began to run up them as fast as he could. Philip and Peter bounded in pursuit.

The comte fled upwards, but knowing there was no escape. An image of the gallows at Tyburn flashed before his eyes. He darted into a bedroom on the second floor and slammed the door, leaning against it, panting, and hearing the heavy thud of footsteps running up to the door outside. He turned the key in the lock and ran to the window and hauled it up. The sun had disappeared and long yellow fingers of fog were beginning to creep along the streets. The door behind him shook as Philip threw his weight against it. Like most people, the comte credited everyone with his own sins. He had tortured and beaten many a victim in his checkered past, and he felt sure there would be little of him left to hang on the gallows by the time Lord Philip was finished with him.

With a final ear-splitting crack the door gave behind him. With a great cry he flung himself from the window and his body hurtled down to the cobbles and lay still, looking like the lifeless puppets on the counter of the now finished Punch and Judy show.

Philip and Peter ran out into the street and slowly turned the comte over. Blood was pouring from a wound in his head and his breath was coming in rapid, fluttering sighs.

Philip knelt down beside him.

'Where is Constance?' he said. 'What have you done with her?'

The comte's black eyes slowly opened, their dying light enlivened by a faint flicker of malice.

'In . . . the . . . river. Dead,' he said. He choked and a stream of blood gushed from his mouth over the cobbles, and the little gleam of malice in his eyes flared up tri-umphantly and then died.

'He's dead,' said Peter, pulling Philip away.

'And so is she,' muttered Philip. 'How shall I live without her now, Peter? How shall I live with myself?'

The news of the comte's perfidy was all over London next day. Peter saw to that. Constance was exonerated. Lady Amelia tried to spread gossip that Constance had been the Comte Duval's mistress and found herself socially ostracized as a result — her dear friend, Mary Besant, making sure everyone knew from whence the rumour had hailed. Dismal, chilly fog lay over the streets of London as if it had come to stay forever. Summer had gone and there had been very little autumn, only a hurried descent into the depths of winter.

Lord Philip's tall figure dressed from head to foot in mourning black became a familiar figure in the streets of London as he walked and walked and walked, only returning to his home late at night to fall into an exhausted and nightmare-ridden sleep.

His grief was aggravated by a persistent feeling that Constance was not dead — that somewhere among all these dark and twisting and fogbound streets, he would find her. Perhaps around the next corner, his mind would torment him.

One night, he wearily returned from one of these long walks and climbed slowly to his room. He was suddenly obsessed with the idea that Constance might have left some clue, some message for him. He had ordered her rooms to be left untouched and, since Bouchard, the lady's maid, had left shortly after Constance's disappearance, no one had been near them.

He walked along the corridor and pushed open the door. All was just as she had left it. Lying on the bed, he saw the frivolous dress and bonnet he had taken objection to. If only she were alive and well, she could wear any damn bonnet in the whole of the world! Overcome with sadness and weariness and loss, he picked up her dress and buried his face in the soft folds. He drew back and stared at the dress with a puzzled frown on his face. Instead of Constance's faint perfume, there was a stale, rank smell of sweat from the dress. Well, it had been a hot day. Still, he frowned, picking up the bonnet and turning it over in his long fingers. Sticking to the inside of the gauze was one reddish brown hair.

He sat down on the bed and stared at it. Constance's hair was midnight black. But where had he seen that colour of hair before? And then he remembered the lady's maid, Bouchard. He rang for Masters.

No, Masters could not recall the mamselle saying she had found new employ. She had just packed her bags and left, which had seemed natural as her job was redundant . . .

Lord Philip looked thoughtfully at the butler.

'Where did we find Bouchard?' he asked. 'Did you employ her?'

Masters thought for a long moment. 'No, my lord. As I recall, it was Mr Evans who employed her. If you remember, my lord, the day before your lordship's wedding, you said as how my lady would need a maid. I could not promise to find anyone suitable at such short notice, and your lordship said you would ask Mr Evans to engage someone.'

Lord Philip pulled out his watch. Past midnight. He could not go calling at this late hour. He would just have to wait until the morning.

'Tell me, Masters,' he said. 'On the day my wife disappeared, you said she returned to the house.'

'Yes, my lord,' said Masters surprised. 'I told . . .'

'Did you see her face?' demanded Philip harshly.

'Well, no, my lord,' said Masters. 'That bonnet you're holding concealed her face.'

'Go rouse the coachman,' said Philip, 'and bring the groom who was on the back strap that day.'

199

He waited impatiently while the servants were ushered in.

The coachman and groom could not remember whether they had seen my lady's face or not. 'But you heard her speak?' demanded Philip in exasperation, 'after she left my sister's house, that is.'

The coachman's great brow was furrowed in thought. Philip felt like shaking him. But it was the groom who answered, a sharp-eyed Cockney.

'My lady didn't say nuffink,' he said ('my lord,' prompted Masters in a scandalized whisper). 'It was that there Mr Evans who told us for to take my lady home . . . me lord,' said the groom, 'being as how she was feeling poorly.'

Philip took a deep breath. 'Now I want all of you to think hard,' he said. 'Could the female you took home have been Bouchard *masquerading* as my lady?'

A shocked silence greeted this. The groom again spoke first. 'I dunno,' he said. 'But there was something, not much . . .'

'Yes?' said Philip impatiently.

'I didn't like 'er,' said the groom. 'I felt I didn't like that there lady in the carriage. I thought the 'eat must've got to me brain 'cos I like 'er ladyship but that there lady . . . I dunno . . . Course I thought it was the 'eat, like, cos I never thought for a moment it wasn't my lady, 'er with that there bonnet and all.'

'I will call on Mr Evans in the morning,' said Lord Philip grimly. 'Not a word of this to anyone.'

Chapter Twelve

Lady Eleanor seemed startled at her brother's urgent request the next day to speak to Mr Evans. The secretary was out, somewhere in the City, with Mr Rider. Both would be returning in time for her *musicale* that afternoon.

Philip went in search of Peter to tell his friend of the latest developments. He finally found Peter just as that gentleman was emerging from the elegant portals of White's in St James's Street. Peter was looking exceedingly fine in a double-breasted redingote with a satin collar. A curly-brimmed beaver sat at a rakish angle on his thick fair hair, and his hussar leather boots gleamed like twin mirrors. The day was raw and chilly, and Peter had his hands thrust into an enormous sealskin muff.

They elected to go to the Wanderers Club, a new and not so fashionable establishment on the fringe of St James's. They settled themselves in the chart room, confident that they would not be disturbed. The rest of the club was empty with the exception of a bunch of Cits playing a tepid game of hazard in the card room.

'Evans!' exclaimed Peter. 'It can't be Evans. He wouldn't hurt a fly.'

'I agree,' said Philip, 'but he could be easily tricked. Anyway, my sister's house is the last place Constance was seen. Before I tackle Evans, I want you to keep him in conversation while I search through his rooms. You know, Peter, I'm so sick and worried and the whole trouble is that I can't believe she's dead. Sometimes I think I'm losing my mind. I *am* losing my mind. There's two green eyes staring at me out of your muff.'

Peter had placed his muff on a small adjoining table. As both men watched, the muff appeared to take on a life of its own and rolled slowly over.

Peter picked it up and shook it. A large tabby cat rolled out, stretched itself, and then proceeded to wash with aristocratic indifference.

'The kitchen cat,' said Peter in disgust. 'It gets everywhere.'

'Do you mean you've been carrying that great mangy thing around in your muff and didn't *know* it?' said Philip.

'Well, it's odd now you mention it,' said Peter looking thoughtfully at the cat. 'I thought it felt unusually soft and warm and heavy. It must have been sleeping the whole time. By Jove, I remember thinking, these muffs are so cunning you would almost think they were breathing. And then, of course at White's, I didn't take off my hat or gloves or anything because it's not the thing to do unless you're staying longer than ten minutes, which I wasn't. Amazingly clever brute that. I had better go home and change for your sister's *musicale*. At least it ain't a rout. Never *can* see anyone at routs. All push and shove on the stairs to get in, and push and shove to get out and the hostess doesn't feel it's been a success unless several people have fainted in the crush, and some poor fellow's carriage has got shattered in the traffic outside.'

'I shall drop you at your lodgings and then call for you in a couple of hours,' said Lord Philip. 'What shall we do with the cat?'

'Leave it here,' said Peter indifferently. 'I don't want it. Do you?'

As Lord Philip left his friend at his lodgings and watched Peter climbing up the stairs, he noticed that the cat was clinging for dear life to the back of Peter's redingote.

He made a movement as if to call after Peter and tell him about the animal, and then changed his mind. Peter would no doubt digress forever on the iniquities of the cat and would probably forget to change his clothes.

The *musicale* had already begun when Peter and Philip walked into Lady Eleanor's mansion. Mr Evans and her husband had not yet returned, she said somewhat crossly. Lady Eleanor had hired a full orchestra for the occasion, and had invited the cream of Society to the event. Lady Amelia was not among the guests. Peter sat himself near the door where he could look into the hall and note when Mr Evans arrived home.

Lord Philip moved quietly up the stairs. He slipped a footman a guinea and asked him to direct him to Mr Evans's private chambers.

The footman led the way to the top of the house. Mr Evans's quarters were comprised of only a small sitting room which led to a sparse cupboard of a bedroom. Lord Philip began to feel ashamed of his suspicions of the meek secretary. Everything in the rooms breathed of respectably straitened circumstances. There were no incriminating letters or papers of any kind. The names of Godwin, Wolstonecraft, Holcroft and Thelwall on the bookshelves showed that the secretary had radical tastes, but that was all. Lord Philip was just about to leave when he noticed the edge of a tin trunk sticking out from under the bed. He felt suddenly grubby, but driven by that recurring nagging feeling that Constance was somehow alive, he pulled it out and opened the lid.

He found himself looking down at a full-dress court outfit which rivalled his own in richness and elegance. Wonderingly, he drew it out. There was a violet satin frock coat with white satin lining, waistcoat and breeches embroidered in gold and green, a set of jewelled buttons, a fine lingerie shirt with cravat and collar points, white silk stockings, black pumps with gold buckles, a black felt bicorne with a white frill, and lastly a dress sword hanging on a broad lilac silk ribbon. Mr Evans had no call to wear court dress. It could not have belonged to, say, a more affluent relative, for it was brand-new and obviously tailored to fit Mr Evans's slim form. Lord Philip felt his eyes drawn to a long looking-glass on the other side of the bedroom. He had a sudden vision of Mr Evans parading in the privacy of his bedroom in full court dress. With a frown he turned again to the jewelled buttons. They were ornamented with tiny diamonds of the first water and deep dark rubies. How on earth could a mere secretary afford such splendour?

I shall go and ask him, thought Lord Philip. Enough of this sneaking about.

He placed the clothes carefully back in the trunk and made his way downstairs.

Mr Evans was just entering the hall with Mr Rider as he reached the bottom step. Philip moved quickly forward. 'A word with you, Mr Evans,' he said. Did the man turn pale — or was that his imagination?

Mr Evans mutely led the way to the small book-lined study at the back of the house.

'Sit down,' commanded Lord Philip. Mr Evans took the chair behind a rococo pedestal desk and stared apprehensively at his visitor. But then, Mr Evans always looked apprehensive.

In a flat emotionless voice, Lord Philip outlined his suspicions of Bouchard, told Mr Evans exactly how the comte had died, and then went on to explain how and why he had searched the secretary's rooms. 'I have no apology to give, other than the fact that I have a feeling my wife is not dead.' He held up his hand as Mr Evans gave a stifled exclamation. 'I did, however, come across an exceedingly fine suit of court clothes. Do you intend being presented, Mr Evans?'

Mr Evans flushed a dull red, and to Lord Philip's acute embarrassment, the secretary's weak eyes filled with tears. 'You had *no right,* no right whatsoever, my lord, to go to my rooms without my permission,' said Mr Evans. 'But I shall tell you how I came by that dress. I went to Newmarket last year, if you will recall, with Mr Rider. I had just received my yearly salary. I was overcome with a strange madness and put it all on Small Beer.'

'I remember Small Beer was a hundred to one,' nodded Lord Philip.

'Exactly. So I had a small fortune. The madness was still on me. I knew I would never be presented at court, never wear it, but I wanted a court dress. I wear it when ... when I am alone,' finished Evans in a low voice.

It was all so pathetic, thought Lord Philip getting to his feet and walking edgily about the room. But Evans had been alone in the house on the day his wife had disappeared. Therefore Evans had been the last to see her — that is, if Bouchard had masqueraded as her. Therefore, Evans had still a few questions to answer. Lord Philip turned his eyes away from the other man's miserable face and stood looking at a George I bureau cabinet. He idly opened down the writing flap, and then closed it again before turning to ask his next question.

Then he slowly turned back, opened the writing flap, lifted it gently down and stared at one of the pigeonholes at the back of the cabinet.

He leaned forward and took out a fan and spread it open, staring at the pretty painted picture of two peacocks promenading on an emerald green lawn. He was transported back to that evening in the library when Constance had fluttered a fan in front of her face. Then he remembered Peter sitting among the refreshments at Almack's, idly fanning himself and then explaining it was Constance's fan.

Lord Philip's eyes began to burn with a murderous light as he turned about and held the fan open in front of the secretary's terrified eyes.

'My wife,' he said grimly. 'What have you done with my wife?'

'*Nothing!*' screamed Mr Evans over the sound of the cascading woodwinds of 'La cambiale di matrimonio' from the *musicale*.

It would be a long time before Lord Philip Cautry could listen to Rossini without a shudder.

Chapter Thirteen

Joe Puddleton took a great swig at his tankard of shrub and looked hopefully round the tap. But he was no longer the focus of attention. The villagers of Upper Comley had lost interest in the poor madwoman in his care, and no one seemed prepared to buy him a drink in order to receive the latest bulletin.

And on this blustery cold day, Joe would have loved to talk, not to be the centre of attention, but to ease a little feeling of anxiety that was beginning to surface in the primeval bog inside his head which passed for a brain. In his slow countryman's way, he mulled over the facts.

The gentleman from London had said his missus was deranged, and deranged she looked with her hair all anyhow and screaming and pleading. She was to be kept fast in Lumley's old cottage down by the river, and no one was to be allowed to come nigh.

Joe had been warned that the poor mad creature was under the impression she was a titled lady with a lord for a husband. He was to take meals to her daily, and check that the bars on the windows and the locks on the doors were secure. On fine days, she was to be allowed out into the small garden at the back of the cottage for a short airing. Several times she had tried to escape only to be foiled by himself, a fact of which he had been very proud, and for which the London gentleman had paid him a bonus.

But of late, the lady had gone very quiet, paying him not much attention, head bent over a piece of sewing. Then, this morning, she had begun to speak to him in a deadly reasonable voice. She had stated that the gentleman who was paying him was a French spy, and that if he did not immediately release her then he would find himself dangling at the end of the nubbing cheat. She had actually said hangman's rope, but Joe had translated that into his own cant.

She had seemed very sane, terrifyingly so. All Joe could do was to wait until the gentleman from London called on one of his rare visits, and see if he could get to the bottom of it.

His musings were interrupted by the

arrival of a stranger who drew out a chair and pulled it up close to his own. In his slow way, Joe disliked the stranger on sight. He had a crafty look, although his sober clothes were of good cut.

But the stranger insisted on buying Joe a quartern of the landlord's best ale, and under its influence Joe looked at the stranger with a more benevolent eye. He only looked a mean cove, decided Joe, because of the strange crabways movements of his long body. By the second tankard, Joe was prepared to slowly move his conversation from the poor harvest and give the generous fellow the story of his strange charge.

The stranger listened with flattering attention, until Joe at last ponderously voiced his doubts as to the lady's insanity. 'I'm a-telling you, Mr . . . er . . . that that there mort sounds as right in 'er 'ead as what you or me does. 'Appen she'm be telling truth.'

But at this fascinating piece of news, the stranger seemed to lose interest, putting his well filled purse away, shrugging himself into his caped carrick, and taking his leave. His lack of interest made Joe think that perhaps he should keep his thoughts about the young lady's sanity to himself. Obviously people would rather hear about a madwoman. By the time he had staggered from

212

the inn, he had convinced himself once more of his charge's madness.

Bergen jumped on his horse and rode hard in the direction of London. He was very worried. He had found himself at a bit of a loss after quitting his employ at Lady Amelia's. Thanks to the sale of the jewels, he had money enough and more. But his plotting nature was restless for lack of interest. He worried and wondered as to the reason for the murder of Lady Philip. And that was how he came to shadow Evans, following the secretary every time he left the house. The secretary's calls and duties seemed boringly respectable, until one evening Bergen had seen him setting out in a hired carriage and had spurred his horse in pursuit.

His pursuit led him to the outskirts of a small village near Hounslow Heath. He watched Evans entering a barred and shuttered cottage. A light had then appeared in the downstairs window in one of the rooms where the old shutters were slightly broken. Bergen had crept up cautiously and put his eye to a crack.

He had nearly fallen back into the garden in amazement. Lady Philip Cautry was sitting in the candlelight talking vehemently to Mr Evans.

Bergen could not make out the words, but the couple seemed to be very companionable together. He felt a cold knot of fear in his stomach. Constance had been unconscious when he had appeared on the scene with Bouchard, but what if Evans had told her about them? Rumours had reached Evans that Lord Philip did not believe his wife dead.

He had decided to wait around and see what news he could pick up. His investigations had led him to Joe. He decided now to go straight to Evans and strangle that gentleman until he told him what he was playing at. If Evans or Constance ever spoke, then he and Bouchard would find themselves on Tyburn tree dangling at the end of a rope.

On reaching town, he called at Bouchard's lodgings in the rabbit warren of Soho. The ex-lady's maid listened to him in growing fear and terror. 'Let us go to Mr Evans immediately,' she cried. 'He owes us some explanation.'

But as they reached Lady Eleanor's house, they were stopped short by the sight of the secretary being dragged down the steps by Lord Philip. In the flare of the flambeaux, the secretary's face was puffy and bruised and tears were running down his cheeks.

The couple drew into the shadows and listened.

'You could have saved yourself a great deal of pain had you told me the whereabouts of my wife in the first place,' Lord Philip was saying. 'You shall conduct me thence, and then I shall turn you over to the authorities. You are a spy and a traitor and shall be treated accordingly.' Lord Philip turned to address Peter Potter who had appeared on the steps of the mansion. 'Peter,' said Lord Philip, 'help me guard this useless piece of carrion until I get my travelling carriage ready.'

Bouchard gripped Bergen's arm. 'That gives us time,' she hissed.

'For what?' queried Bergen, his face like a death mask in the flickering shadows.

'Don't you see?' said Bouchard desperately. 'It's either them or us. We must kill them all.'

'You're mad,' shivered Bergen. 'How can we?'

'Get to the cottage first,' whispered Bouchard, 'and when they're all inside, bar the doors and set fire to it.'

'What of Cautry's servants?' exclaimed Bergen. 'D'ye think they're going to stand back and watch us burn their master to death?'

'Fool! I shall get rid of them. Come, monsieur, I repeat — them or us. Do you think they will forget about us? Cautry will have every Runner scouring the countryside for us!'

'Quickly, then,' said Bergen, pointing with his weighted walking stick to two fine mounts tethered outside Lady Eleanor's mansion. 'Those will do. Can you ride?'

'Of course,' said Bouchard. 'To save my neck I can do anything, *mon bonhomme. Vite!*'

Somewhere in Constance's long imprisonment, the half frightened, rather immature girl had disappeared leaving an angry desperate woman. On each of his brief visits, usually during the dark hours of the night, Mr Evans had been adamant. She would never escape, and must think herself lucky that he was a humane man and could not bring himself to kill her.

She had listened in growing dismay to his revelations. He believed in Napoleon Bonaparte as the saviour of England. When the Emperor took his rightful place at St James's, the old effete aristocracy would be put to the guillotine and be replaced by the new — which would of course be comprised of men like himself. Mr Evans had a vivid imagination, and his favourite dream seemed to be the one where Lady Eleanor was borne through the jeering crowds on a tumbril to have her haughty head lopped off.

The comte's suicide had moved him greatly, and he also dreamed of erecting a monument to the 'martyr'. All this nonsense seemed at odds with the secretary's usual timid bearing and correct manner. Constance had at first wept and pleaded with him, but under the secretary's timid exterior burned the fires of the zealot.

So Constance passed her weary days dreaming of her handsome husband, and often wondering how she had ever had the temerity to be rude to such a god. Only let her be safely back in his arms again, and he could choose her whole wardrobe if he liked and never, never would she raise her voice to him again.

Mr Evans had bragged about his cunning in finding Bergen and Bouchard. Constance had not been at all surprised at the part taken in the plot by the sinister Bergen, but had been amazed at the evil of her own lady's maid.

'I had that one marked out a long time ago,' Evans had said proudly. 'Bouchard was once a lady's maid before your employ, and lost her job then. She was suspected of taking her employer's jewels, although nothing could be proved against her. No, she does not believe in our cause. She is simply a low type of woman who will do anything for money.'

'And what of Joe Puddleton?' Constance had asked.

Oh, Joe was nothing more than a village bumpkin, Evans had replied, with an aristocratic dismissal quite foreign, surely, to his democratic principles. Constance's hopes had risen, and she had commenced her appeals to her jailer for help. But until this very morning, the stolid Joe had appeared to treat all her cries for help with great good humour and two large, deaf cauliflower ears.

The cottage in which she was imprisoned was built of wattle and half timbered. It had a heavy thatched roof. A small garden at the back was enclosed on both sides by high impregnable thorn hedges, and bordered on a swift river.

She looked out of the window at the front of the house at the cold wind sweeping across the stubble of the fields, and awaited the return of Joe.

The cottage consisted of two rooms, one for sleeping and one for eating. A small kitchen had been added to the back.

Constance kept her prison well scrubbed and dusted. It was very cold that day, and Constance sat with a blanket wrapped around her shoulders and debated which of the sparse pieces of furniture she should break up for firewood should Joe fail to bring any of the promised logs.

On days like this, she began to fear that Mr Evans would succeed in keeping her locked away from the world forever. Would Philip be searching for her? Or would he console himself as he had done in the past with some available lightskirt? The thought of Philip in another woman's arms made her feel slightly sick, and she closed her eyes in pain.

The wind howled and moaned in the chimney, and Constance turned her gaze back to the window. In the bare fields opposite, she remembered, she had watched the men gathering in the harvest and had beat against the barred windows, yelling and screaming until her voice was hoarse and her hands had bled. They had turned their heads away in a sort of embarrassed manner, and Constance realized hopelessly that, like Joe, they all considered her mad.

The burly figure of Joe appeared in view, carrying a basket and struggling with the large key to the cottage door which he kept tucked into his belt.

A wave of excitement suddenly crept over Constance. What if she were to stand behind the door with, say, the poker, and stun the man as he entered?

Desperate for freedom, she seized the brass poker and pressed herself against the wall behind the door.

Joe Puddleton stood on the threshold of the little parlour and stared about. 'Now where mun 'er be . . .' he began when Constance brought the poker down on his head with all the force she could muster.

Joe swung round scratching his head. 'There was no call for ee to do that,' he said, blinking stupidly at Constance who flung herself into a chair and began to weep miserably. The poker had made not the slightest dent in his thick skull.

Joe put the basket of food on the table. 'I thought ee was a reasonable mort for all ee's mad,' accused Joe. 'But to hit a man with a poker ain't fair.'

Almost sulkily, he turned and walked from the cottage, carefully bolting the door behind him, indifferent to Constance's sobs.

After a long time Constance dried her eyes and settled back again into her usual mood of quiet resignation and despair.

There was no clock in the cottage, so all she could do to measure the hours on a sunless day such as this was to wait and wait until the grey light faded to black, heralding the end of another weary day.

Usually she retired to bed as soon as darkness fell but this evening, for some odd reason, she felt as restless as the wind outside. The night seemed alive with strange noises. There were often noises of various wild animals, foxes, weasels, rabbits pursuing each other in their endless hunt, and the sudden hoot of an owl. But the scurryings outside seemed to hold a breathless menace. Almost as if *people* were scurrying around the cottage, thought Constance. There was also an increasingly strong smell of lamp oil, and she carefully trimmed the lamp and then sniffed at it but it seemed to be burning brightly enough. Joe had returned that evening to bar the shutters of the window of the living-room as he did every evening, not trusting to the iron bars across the windows alone.

If I ever see him again, thought Constance for the hundredth time, conjuring up a picture of her handsome husband, not one word of criticism will I utter. Not one harsh word. Only please let him find me.

The scurryings outside ceased, the wind

died down, and the night was very still.

Then she heard the sounds of horses' hooves.

There was a creak of carriage wheels and the confused sound of voices.

'*Help!*' screamed Constance, louder than she had ever done before.

There came an answering shout, and the rapid sound of footsteps hurrying over the hard, frozen earth outside the cottage.

'Well, where's the key, man?' demanded a well beloved voice.

'All in good time, me lord,' said Joe Puddleton's voice. 'I got un right here.'

My lord!

Hardly daring to hope or breathe, Constance ran to the cottage door. There was a maddening fumbling at the lock, and then the cottage door swung open.

Lord Philip Cautry flanked by Peter Potter and Joe Puddleton stood on the threshold.

'Is there anyone else with you?' asked Philip.

Constance shook her head and took a faltering step forward. Philip moved to meet her and caught his wife in his arms.

'So she was a lady after all,' said Joe wonderingly. 'Better than a raree show, this is.'

'Turn your back, man!' cried Peter. 'Turn

your back!' as Lord Philip bent his head to kiss his wife.

Lord Philip's servants waited outside in his carriage, ready to dash to his rescue if need be. But all at the cottage seemed quiet. The coachman and the two grooms were feeling sleepy and tired, and wished his lordship would get on with it and let them all go home.

They did not see the dark figure of Bouchard, creeping up along the hedgerow.

In the next minute, a huge firecracker sparked and exploded right under the horses' hooves. The terrified animals reared and plunged and then bolted in headlong flight. At the same time, Bergen slammed the cottage door shut and rolled a large rock, which he had ready for the purpose, against the low door so that it wedged under the latch, holding it shut. He lit a torch and stood ready and then turned a white face to Bouchard who had come running up. 'I c-can't do it,' he stammered. 'Not all of 'em. *I can't!*'

'Let me,' snapped Bouchard with a grim impatience worthy of Lady Macbeth telling her husband to screw his courage to the sticking place. 'I had banked on that fool Evans being with him. We must finish this work and speed back to London and see if we can stop his mouth.'

She seized a torch and applied it to the brushwood soaked in lamp oil which she and Bergen had piled against the walls of the cottage a bare half hour before Lord Philip's arrival.

With a satisfying roar, the brushwood went up, the long flames licking at the overhanging thatch.

Bergen stood back, shivering despite the heat of the fire. He could imagine the terrified captives inside, running helplessly from flaming wall to flaming wall, and then their bodies crackling and sizzling like a pig turning on a spit over the kitchen fire. As he felt the bile rising in his throat, he remembered he had forgotten to wedge the back door. And that great lummox called Joe had the key! He turned to tell Bouchard. That lady was standing with her arms folded, and a grim and awful smile of satisfaction on her face. 'I shan't tell her,' he thought beginning to edge away.

Bouchard caught the movement and swung round and stared at the white, twitching face of the ex-butler. Bouchard herself felt no more than a heady excitement at the deed she had just done. The fear and disgust she saw on Bergen's face meant only one thing to her — betrayal.

She drew a cumbersome pistol from the folds of her long drab coat, and with as little pity as certain of her countrywomen, some decades ago, had watched the heads toll from the guillotine into the basket beneath, she raised the pistol and shot Bergen through the heart. And as the man swayed and stumbled, she raised one serviceably-booted foot and kicked him so hard that he fell back into the roar of the fire just as the roof collapsed.

The halloos and cries of Lord Philip's returning servants spurred her to flight.

At the back of the cottage, Constance, Philip, Peter and Joe huddled on the damp grass beside the river, and watched in awe as the cottage roared and blazed.

There was nothing they could do but watch. There was no way through the thick hedges at either side, and the river behind them was swift and deep.

Philip held Constance close, his heart full of gratitude for their escape, for the stupidity of their would-be murderers in failing to secure the back door.

At long last the flames died down and the anxious faces of the servants could be seen through the blackened ruins of the cottage on the other side. The cottage was too far away from the village for anyone to have seen the flames and to have come to help put out the fire.

Joe Puddleton finally picked his way through the ruins and found an iron bucket and carried it back to the river. He filled it with water, and then returning to the burned house, began to soak a path across the scorching rubble so that his new aristocratic friends could make their way out.

Peter finally led the way with Philip carrying Constance in his arms behind him. 'Mind your step, me lords,' said Joe bowing low and elevating Peter to the peerage. As he bent, his large eye fell on what appeared to be a hand sticking out from under a beam and a pile of rubble. " 'Ere!' he said slowly. " 'Ere's a corp.'

He began kicking away the rubble. 'Let me get my wife out of this first,' snapped Philip, but it was too late. Joe's massive foot had turned aside the debris to reveal the scorched and blackened face of what was still disgustingly recognizable as Bergen.

The coachmen and the grooms eagerly helped their master out into the front garden.

'It was that there lady's maid, my lord,' cried the coachman. 'She must have been the one. Set a firecracker under our horses' feet so that they bolted. When I'd calmed them down and ridden back, we saw her escaping. We saw her face in the flames.'

'Bergen and Bouchard,' said Philip slowly. 'Well, Bergen's dead but Bouchard still lives, and I'll get that hell-witch if I have to search the length and breadth of England.'

Constance felt numb and stunned by the horrifying events of the night. She clung on to her husband, staring up repeatedly at his face as if he was some dear ghost who would surely vanish at cockcrow.

'What did you do with Evans?' asked Philip of Peter Potter as the coach rumbled back to London. Constance had fallen into an exhausted sleep.

In the flaring light from the carriage lamps, Peter's face took on an almost guilty expression. 'Well, you know,' he said reluctantly, 'Your sister can be quite a formidable lady.'

'What has that to do with it?' demanded Philip, holding Constance's slight body against his own as the carriage lurched and swayed over the frozen ruts of the road.

'I was going to lock him up . . . you know . . . when you went off to get your travelling carriage . . . but Lady Eleanor appeared out on the street and began to screech and demand to know what was going on. So I told her. So she says the scandal Mr Rider will have to suffer will be too much if I hand him over to the authorities, so she insists that Evans be taken back into the house and locked in his room until you return.'

'Fool!' said Philip bitterly.

'I say, don't be like that,' said Peter, feeling that his friend's acid tone was poor repayment for his night's help.

'I'm sorry, Peter,' said Lord Philip wearily. 'I'll talk some sense into Eleanor's snobbish head as soon as I get Constance safely home. Bouchard is still somewhere about. I don't think she will try to harm Constance now, but I would like my wife guarded at all times just the same. We shall take Constance with us to Eleanor's,' added his lordship with singularly masculine insensitivity. 'She should have a chance to tell him to his face what she thinks of him.'

'You can't do that!' cried Peter, outraged. 'Think what the poor girl has been through. She should go straight home and into bed with a hot posset.'

'Fustian,' said Philip coldly. 'Constance is not one of your milk and water misses. Did you not notice how remarkably *well* she looked despite her imprisonment?'

Peter shook his head as if in disbelief, but fell silent.

A red dawn was bathing the cobbles in a fiery light as the coach wearily pulled to a stop outside Lady Eleanor's mansion.

Constance awoke with a little cry of fear and then smiled sheepishly as she looked up into her husband's face. 'Oh, it will be so lovely to be home,' she sighed.

'We're not going home just yet,' said Philip gently. 'Evans must be delivered into the hands of the authorities, but I am sure you would like to give him a piece of your mind first.'

'But I did,' wailed Constance, 'give him a piece of my mind, that is. Every time I saw him!'

But Lord Philip was cursed with the demon of nagging jealousy. Constance had looked so *well*, so beautiful when he had found her. He did not realize that Constance had simply worked hard on her clothes and on her appearance to keep up her morale, and to encourage her hopes of him finding her. Philip simply wanted to see her face to face with Evans. After all, what had gone on in that secluded little cottage? Evans had had a very beautiful young girl in his power for quite some time. And Evans was surely a man like any other under that rabbit-like facade . . .

He paid no attention to Constance's

sleepy protests, but roused the sleeping servants and climbed up to the top of the house to Mr Evans's rooms, after having secured the key from the butler.

He took a candle from a small table in the corridor outside, lit it, and held it up. He handed the key to Peter who inserted it in the lock and slowly and cautiously opened the door.

'Now, Evans . . .' began Lord Philip, striding into the room and holding the candle high.

From a hook on the low ceiling dangled what was left of Mr Evans. He was dressed in his full court uniform, and the candle sent sparks and prisms of light from the jewels of his buttons on to his sad and swollen face. The secretary had hanged himself with the pretty, lilac silk sword sash. His little black pumps with their brave gold buckles swung a bare inch above the floor.

There was a sigh and a moan from behind Lord Philip. He swung round. Brave Constance who had endured so many trials and tribulations with such fortitude had finally had too much.

She had fainted dead away.

Chapter Fourteen

Constance had contracted a feverish cold and had been confined to her bed for a fortnight.

The body of Evans had been quietly removed and quietly interred. The Cautry family had suffered enough scandal, and, after all, with the exception of Bouchard who seemed to have disappeared into thin air, the rest of the participants in the plot were dead.

Lord Philip Cautry's pride had toppled from a great height. He looked back on his behaviour that terrible evening and thought he must have run mad. To have found Constance again, to have been able to hold her in his arms again, only to become unreasonably jealous and subject her to the dreadful sight of the secretary's suicide, was beyond belief. He was not even fit to touch the hem of her gown. He went quietly and sadly about his home, questioning the physician closely after that man's daily visits, but not daring to visit the sickroom himself in case the sight of his monstrous bullying face gave his delicate wife a relapse.

Anxious and worried, Peter told him he was behaving like the veriest fool going to such extremes, to which Lord Philip had crossly answered that Peter was ill-suited to talk of fools, parading, as he was, around London with that curst cat.

Peter had developed a fondness for the kitchen cat. It was bad enough, said Lord Philip, to have Frederick 'Poodle' Byng driving about with his poodle beside him and Lord Petersham breaking out in a rash of brown — brown clothes, brown carriage and brown horses, and all for the love of a Mrs Brown — without his best friend making a cake of himself by squiring about the kitchen cat.

It was an ill-favoured beast with a dusty striped coat and an insolent green eye. Kept to its proper position of keeping down the population of rats and mice in its master's kitchen, it was all very well. But sitting in Peter's carriage with a brass collar around its neck, it was making its master an object of ridicule.

But Peter and his cat seemed oblivious to

232

remarks and stares alike. The cat had not yet been blessed with a name and became known in London Society as 'Potter's Familiar' and some wag circulated a poem in its honour:

'Potter's Familiar is seen in the Park
Potter's Familiar at Almack's is found
Potter's Familiar is seen after dark
At the Opera, in jewels, exquisitely gown'd.
What female can hope to capture the heart
Of a fellow whose life is all for — *a Cat!*'

Peter and Philip strolled into Lord Philip's mansion one foggy afternoon and found Constance lying on a chaise longue in the drawing-room. She looked very pale and ethereal.

'My constant companion,' murmured Lord Philip bending over her head. Constance's face took on a closed, tight look and he drew his hand away, thinking he disgusted her. Constance had merely resented the term 'companion' which had such unhappy memories for her. Peter's cat lazily climbed on to her lap by dint of pulling itself up her thin muslin dress by all of its claws.

Philip strode forward and picked it up by

the scruff of the neck and dropped it on the floor, where it lay with its tail lashing and its green eyes glaring through the bands of fog that lay in layers in the stuffy air of the dark room.

'Leave the cat alone,' said Constance, with a slight edge to her voice. 'It is only behaving naturally, after all. Or did you expect it to make a bow first and leave its calling card?'

'Oh, if you *want* the curst fleabag, then *have* it!' said Lord Philip reaching out a hand for the cat, which promptly scratched him, and then climbed its way up Peter's long body to crouch on his shoulder.

Peter looked hopefully from one to the other of the married pair. What they needed, he decided, was a good row to clear the air.

But Constance remembered her vow to be a meek and obedient wife, and at the same time Philip felt like a boor and became extremely solicitous and courteous. The married couple then proceeded to talk over the tea tray as if they were strangers meeting for the first time at some court function.

'My sister is giving a *musicale*,' said Lord Philip at length. 'I told her you would not wish to go. Her house must hold very sad memories for you, and you should not go out in this weather. You still look very frail.'

'Thank you for your concern, sir,' said Constance meekly. 'But I should like very much to go. I am feeling much stronger and I think some amusement would do me good.'

'But . . .' Lord Philip began to protest while Peter hopefully pricked up his ears. To Peter's disappointment, Lord Philip only stood frowning for a few seconds, and then said in a mild voice, 'Very well. I will tell my sister to expect us. Remind me to ask Masters about how to go about hiring you a lady's maid . . .'

'I already have one,' said Constance. 'Had you visited me when I was unwell, my lord, then you would have noticed her.'

'I did not visit you in your sickroom,' said Lord Philip testily, 'because I feared my face would bring back too many painful memories.'

'I have no painful memories of you,' said Constance. 'But I often wonder what became of Bouchard. When I look out of the window, I seem to see her.'

'Do not worry,' said Peter, 'Bouchard left the country long ago, I'll be bound.'

Bouchard had in fact managed to be put ashore in France by a smugglers' boat operating out of Devon. The villainous captain had demanded a great deal of money for the journey, but Bouchard estimated she still had plenty left and promised herself a night at the best inn in Boulogne. Then she would make her way to Paris and return to her old employment as lady's maid.

But rich as she felt herself to be, Bouchard presented a sorry appearance when she walked into the comfortably furnished entrance hall of the Homme Qui Rit at Boulogne.

The crossing had been rough, and her clothes were stained with salt water. Her battered bonnet was askew on her head, and she carried only one bandbox.

Drooping with fatigue, Bouchard could hardly take in the rough treatment of the landlord. 'On your way,' this individual said, 'we've no room for the likes of you.'

Bouchard drew herself up, and opened the strings of her reticule and spilled a handful of gold on to a small table in the hall. 'I have gold and more to pay for my room,' she said haughtily. 'I desire your best bedroom and a private parlour.'

Bouchard did not realize she had spoken in English. The landlord stared at the gold as if hypnotized. 'Very good, my lady,' he replied, elevating his strange guest to the peerage. 'You have my sincere apologies, my lady, but in these rough times a poor man has to be careful. My name is Moulier, Monsieur Henri Moulier, at your service . . .'

He led the way up the stairs, talking all the time while Bouchard grimly followed.

She was almost too tired to eat the splendid meal set in front of her an hour later, and after only tasting a little of it, she rose wearily to her feet and left the cosy private parlour to go to her bedchamber.

The sheets were clean, although patched and darned. In fact, thought Bouchard wearily as she removed her bonnet, the whole inn had the appearance of a stage set. It looked very luxurious at first, but as one looked closer, one could see the threadbare reality underneath.

She splashed water on her face and stared at her reflection in the looking glass. It was a pity my lord's servants had seen her face in the glare of the flames, otherwise she would not have had to flee. Bouchard believed Constance and her rescuers to have perished in the blazing cottage. She thought no more of their deaths than she used to think of the feelings of the pig squealing under her knife on her father's tiny farm in the Loire Valley all those years ago — before she took the dusty road to Paris to find her fortune, and then the even longer road to London.

It was wonderful to be back in her own country and with her own people, instead of waiting hand and foot on those cold-blooded English.

As she stared in the looking glass, the door behind her slowly opened and her eyes dilated with terror as she saw the figure of Monsieur Moulier, the landlord. He was holding a musket and it was pointing straight at her back.

'Do not turn round,' he said in careful English. And as Bouchard leaned on the washstand and stared at his reflection in the looking glass, Monsieur Moulier shot her neatly in the back.

Monsieur Moulier cocked his head to one side and listened as the echoes of the shot reverberated through the inn. But apart from the late Bouchard, it was empty of guests. Then he could hear the shrill voice of his wife telling the servants to go back to bed and mind their own business. He walked forward and picked up Bouchard's reticule and emptied out the gold, stowing it carefully in his pockets.

'What shall we do with her?' hissed his wife's voice suddenly from the doorway. 'Shall we bury the body on the beach or hide it in some alley?'

'No, my love,' said the landlord. 'Help me

carry her into the innyard at the back and place the body against the far fence. We shot her when she was trying to escape, you see. That way we will be heroes, and no one will wonder why she had no money.'

'You're mad!' said his wife, averting her eyes from the spreading pool of blood on the floor. 'How will we be heroes?'

'Why,' grinned her husband, 'we shot an English spy trying to escape. The servants heard her talk English. So do not fuss, *ma petite,* and help me with this carcass.'

'The gold will help us to keep our inn operating until times are easier. Come, she was nothing but a dirty English spy,' he said, beginning to believe his lie.

'That is all. An English spy . . .'

Unaware that justice had been done, in a way, Constance settled down on the morning of the day of the Riders' *musicale* to consult her dressmaker, Madame Vernée.

That grand mistress of the world of fashion had called in person to show Lady Philip examples of all the current fripperies her ladyship might have missed during her illness.

Constance stared down at a sketch. The lady in the picture was wearing an extremely short dress, almost to mid-calf, under which protruded a pair of lacy trousers. 'What on earth is that?' asked Constance.

Madame Vernée allowed herself the luxury of a patronizing titter. 'That is all the crack, my lady,' she said. 'Those —' pointing to the trousers — 'are pantalets. They tie at the knee and one wears them with a chemise dress. I have, by chance, one here to show you. It was made for Lady Jessington who is laid down with her lungs — this fog, my lady, will it *never* go away? — and as she is *exactly* your size, I took the liberty of bringing it along.' She waved an imperious hand, and one of her assistants opened a box and spread out the contents on the sofa. The dress was of pink satin ending in three lacy frills at the hem. The pantalets were of the same material, and also had three lacy frills at the ankle of each leg. Long silk ribbons were threaded through the tops.

It was a ridiculous fashion. 'I should feel as if I were dressed in my underthings only,' said Constance, but she could not help staring at the lacy confection. It was so outrageous, so feminine, so far away from a world of murder and intrigue.

'And yet,' she mused aloud, 'it is strangely becoming. I think after all I shall take it, madame. Are you sure I shall not look too strange?'

'Anyone who is *anyone* in London wears pantalets,' said Madame Vernée stoutly.

But, alas for Constance! the fashion was very new indeed. It appeared that 'anyone who was anyone' was certainly not gracing the *musicale*. Her husband had said he would join her later, and therefore she had been escorted by Peter Potter, complete with Familiar. Peter had kept assuring Constance that he too was in the habit of forgetting to put on all of his clothes, and only looked doubtful when Constance explained it was the latest fashion.

But the men at the *musicale* seemed to find Constance's new ensemble vastly alluring, and some became embarrassingly *warm* in their attentions. Some of the young matrons were openly admiring and envious, but the older women, Lady Eleanor in particular, gave Constance's pantalets one outraged stare before turning their gaze elsewhere as if shying away from a social indiscretion.

Constance could only be glad when the *musicale* started. She wished her husband would arrive before she would have to rise from her chair again and mingle with the other guests. She felt embarrassingly conspicuous and very much alone. Peter had taken his leave. Lady Eleanor had insisted that the Familiar be banished to the kitchen, and so Peter had gone too, although his hostess had pointed out acidly that he could just as well sit in his own kitchens at home, and anyone who made such a cake of themselves over a mere cat must have windmills in his head.

The inevitable strains of Rossini glissaded and cascaded round the room, which was slowly filling up with fog. Every crescendo in the music was met by a perfect volley of coughs from the audience who were, of course, too well bred to cough during the pianissimo bits, and had saved the relief of their maddeningly tickling throats for the loud parts.

At last the overture was over, and all the guests found their coughs had mysteriously disappeared only to return with redoubled force as the heavy strains of Bach began to fill the room.

The yellow fog continued to seep into the room until the musicians at the other end from where Constance was sitting became a blur. The ghostly features of Mr Rider's new secretary loomed up out of the fog. He looked exactly like the late Evans and Constance shuddered. Mr Rider had stubbornly refused to believe Mr Evans's treachery.

Without turning her head, she knew

somehow that her husband had entered the room, and heaved a little sigh of relief. She would sit and dream of the Philip who had made love to her and forget about the stately and correct husband he had now become.

Peter emerged from the kitchens below stairs with his cat under his arm. Peter had eaten half an enormous game pie, washed down with small beer, and the cat had dined on a mountain of fishheads. Both were feeling comfortable and sleepy.

He felt reluctant to venture out into the fog and stood irresolute at the top of the stairs for a few minutes. He yawned as the heavy cat stirred sleepily on his arm. 'I'm tired too,' said Peter. 'Let's find a cosy place to have a snooze.'

He ambled up the stairs and pushed open the door of the library. A cheerful fire crackled on the hearth. 'This will do us nicely, cat,' said Peter. He heard the sound of a step in the corridor outside and frowned. It would be just like Eleanor, he thought, to come barging in screeching about the cat. He saw a large lacquered screen in one corner of the room. He pulled it slightly forward, and put one of the most comfortable chairs behind it, after placing the cat on the floor. He sank into the chair, after making sure that anyone peering into the room would think it was empty, and closed his eyes. The cat jumped on to his lap and performed a sleepy dance with its claws on his waistcoat and then it, too, fell asleep.

The *musicale* drew to an end, and the guests began to stretch and move about before making their way into the adjoining salon where refreshments were to be served.

Lord Philip Cautry could not believe his eyes. Like a vision in the middle of the fog-filled room stood his wife, and as far as he could make out, she was dressed only in her underwear.

He strode forward and seized her arm in a strong grip, and hustled her from the room.

'Don't say anything! Don't even speak,' he raged, 'until I get you somewhere private.'

Puzzled but unresisting, Constance allowed herself to be marched up the stairs and into the library.

'Now, madame,' grated Philip. 'Perhaps you will explain what you are doing in the middle of my sister's *musicale* dressed in nothing but your petticoat . . . and what are those?' he added furiously, pointing to Constance's lacy pantalets.

'Oh, *Philip,*' sighed Constance, 'it is only the latest fashion and . . .' She had been about to explain that she herself felt it was a trifle extreme, but her husband went on to say, 'How dare you! I told you not to choose clothes without my approval!'

And Constance suddenly forgot all her solemn vows to be a meek and obedient wife.

'Pooh!' she said.

'Is that all you have to say?' demanded her husband. He himself looked very elegant and formal as he gazed down at the top of his wife's now bent head. He was dressed in a formal habit — chocolate brown frock coat, drill breeches, white waistcoat and cravat, and white silk stockings with black pumps.

'I never really noticed your hair before,' said Constance momentarily diverted by the sight of her husband's short locks. 'Vastly becoming.'

'Do not try to change the subject,' said Philip. 'What manner of woman are you, madam, to parade yourself in such clothes? You look like the veriest Cyprian.'

'Well, you should know!' said Constance, 'considering your long and intimate acquaintanceship with ladies of that class.'

Lord Philip put one hand on his hip and stared coldly at his wife. 'We will get nowhere by this senseless bickering,' he said.

'I shall ring for a servant and tell him to fetch my sister immediately. She will lend you something suitable . . .'

'Don't touch that bell!' said Constance. 'You will not humiliate me in front of your sister. God knows, you have humiliated me enough yourself without calling in help.'

'Don't be so silly,' said her husband in a now calm, reasonable voice which was more maddening to Constance than all his anger. He reached his hand towards the bellrope. Constance caught it and tried to drag him away.

Furious again, he seized her by the shoulders and began to shake her. Her long black hair came tumbling about her shoulders, and her wide hazel eyes glared at him.

'Oh, Constance,' he said abruptly and bent his mouth to kiss her. She tried to push him away, but the feel of the hard lips and hard body against her own brought memory flooding back. With one hand wound into her hair to keep her mouth pressed against his own, he wrestled frantically at his cravat with the other.

Constance finally freed her mouth and whispered, *'Here?* I-I m-mean . . . you can't want to . . .'

'Oh, yes I can,' said Philip, lowering her on to the floor. His hand ran down the

246

length of her body making her shiver, and stopped at the lace of the pantalets. 'Do these peculiar things go very far up?' he whispered with his mouth against her breast.

'Only as far as the knee.'

'Good,' said Lord Philip Cautry, 'because I mean to go so much further than that. How easily they come undone! Perhaps a sensible fashion after all.'

Peter Potter awoke. Someone had extinguished all the candles but the red glow from the fire revealed that he had something white and lacy lying on his chest. He picked it up and peered at it. By Jove, if it wasn't like one of those peculiar things Constance had had round her ankles. Suddenly coming fully awake, he sat up and pushed his cat from his lap and looked around. Yes, there was another one lying beside his chair. And what were all those clothes doing hanging over the screen? Oh, dear! It couldn't be . . . they couldn't. He applied one eye to the hinge of the screen and turned as red as the glowing fire. They had, by George!

As silently as his cat, he crept from the room.

We hope you have enjoyed this Large Print book. Other Thorndike Press or Chivers Press Large Print books are available at your library or directly from the publishers.

For more information about current and upcoming titles, please call or write, without obligation, to:

Thorndike Press
295 Kennedy Memorial Drive
Waterville, ME 04901 USA
Tel. (800) 223-6121

OR

Chivers Press Limited
Windsor Bridge Road
Bath BA2 3AX
England
Tel. (0225) 335336

All our Large Print titles are designed for easy reading, and all our books are made to last.